Weird Tales ®

SPRING 2010 ▪ VOL. 65, NO. 1

SUBSCRIBE AT WWW.WEIRDTALES.NET

WEIRD TALES was the *first* storytelling magazine devoted explicitly to the realm of the **dark and fantastic.**

Founded in 1923, WEIRD TALES provided a literary home for such diverse wielders of the imagination as **H.P. Lovecraft** (creator of Cthulhu), **Robert E. Howard** (creator of Conan the Barbarian), **Margaret Brundage** (artistic godmother of goth fetishism), and **Ray Bradbury** (author of *The Illustrated Man* and *Something Wicked This Way Comes*).

Today, O wondrous reader of the 21st century, we continue to seek out that which is most weird and unsettling, for your own edification and alarm.

FICTION

LOVE, MUST | Kurt Kirchmeier   **26**
In which a mechanical beast finds something in common with its fleshier counterparts.

HUNGRY GHOSTS | Jay Lake   **34**
In which Old World spirits are not fond of the New.

GINGERBREAD HOUSE | Kater Cheek   **40**
In which dinner is no longer a time for togetherness.

DEDALUS & THE LABYRINTH | J.M. McDermott   **50**
In which death comes from above every day.

AS RECORDED ON BRASS CYLINDERS: ADAGIO FOR TWO DANCERS   **56**
James L. Grant & Lisa Mantchev | In which a clockwork world crushes many hearts.

POETRY

FINAL FLIGHT OF THE SAGITTARIUS RISING   **78**
Samantha Henderson

UTTERANCES | Christina Springer   **80**

EDITORIAL & CREATIVE DIRECTOR Stephen H. Segal   FICTION EDITOR Ann VanderMeer
CONTRIBUTING EDITORS Amanda Gannon, Kenneth Hite, Darrell Schweitzer
ASSISTANT EDITOR/ONLINE Vanessa Ellis   EDITOR EMERITUS George H. Scithers
EDITORIAL ASSISTANTS Colin Azariah-Kribbs, Tessa Kum
CONTRIBUTING ARTISTS Steven Archer, Ming Doyle, Ira Marcks, Paul Sizer, Asya Yordanova

PUBLISHER John Gregory Betancourt   ADVERTISING SALES Evelyn Kriete

ALL WRITERS OF SUCH STORIES ARE PROPHETS

SPECIAL FEATURE
STEAMPUNK SPECTACULAR

12 Book of the Century
In *Boneshaker,* Cherie Priest's epic earth-moving adventure, the Civil War burns in the skies while zombies take Seattle.

17 Boilerplate: The Secret Mechanical Man
Weird Tales presents an exclusive excerpt from steampunk's newest bible: the biography of Boilerplate, America's "first" robot, who really cranked up the 19th century.

DEPARTMENTS

6 | THE BAZAAR | recycled spirits of iron and wood
8 | THE LIBRARY | *The Sad Tale of the Brothers Grossbart*
31 | HARVEY PELICAN & CO. | special offers from the esoterica king
74 | LOST IN LOVECRAFT | the horror of an inverted Bethlehem

COVER ILLUSTRATION | "My Own Heart" by Molly Crabapple

WWW.MOLLYCRABAPPLE.COM

Issue #355

WEIRD TALES ® is published by Wildside Press, LLC. Postmaster and others: send all changes of address and other subscription matters to Wildside Press, 9710 Traville Gateway Dr. #234, Rockville MD 20850–7408. Single copies, $6.99 in U.S.A. & possessions; $10 by first class mail elsewhere. Subscriptions: 4 issues $20 in U.S.A. & possessions; $40 elsewhere, in U.S. funds. Single-copy orders should be addressed to WEIRD TALES at the address above. Copyright © 2009 by Wildside Press, LLC. All rights reserved; reproduction prohibited without prior permission. Typeset & printed in the United States of America. WEIRD TALES ® is a registered trademark owned by Weird Tales, Limited.

The eyrie

Steampunk Specialness, Hammered Together the Weird Tales Way!

BY ANN VANDERMEER

COME CLOSER . . . smell the oil in the gears . . . come on . . . you know you want to.

Welcome to our Spring Steampunk Spectacular! It seems like everywhere you look, someone is doing something steampunk; whether it's a steampunk story, music, clothing, jewelry or art.

And why should *Weird Tales* be any different? As a matter of fact, if you looked into our past, you'd find the magazine publishing some early steampunk back in the day—only we didn't have the name for it yet, so we just called it weird. This issue is no different: We've got all kinds of strangeness for you this time around, and while not every story is steampunk by the book, each one is odd in its own way.

Kurt Kirchmeier shows us that even mechanical beasts can have deep emotional feelings that manifest in physical ways in "Love, Must." We are introduced to the ugly side of reality television in "Gingerbread House" by Kater Cheek. Very creepy— I guarantee you won't look at baking the same way after reading this one.

Jay Lake offers a ghost story, but a ghost story unlike any other, with "Hungry Ghosts." (Perhaps they'd like some gingerbread?) J.M. McDermott's "Dedalus and the Labyrinth" shows you what one person can do to help youngsters navigate the goblins that plague us in life's giant maze.

And James L. Grant & Lisa Mantchev light up this issue with a steampunk novelette extraordi-

naire; spies, cool contraptions and true love. Who could ask for anything more than "As Recorded on Brass Cylinders: Adagio for Two Dancers?"

All this wonderfulness wrapped in a Molly Crabapple cover, and with amazing interior art by the likes of Ming Doyle (whose scrumptious linework called out to us years ago on the Project: Rooftop blog) and Paul Sizer (for whose furiously elegant design skills we thank the grand, steampunk-flavored mess of controlled anarchy that is Warren Ellis's Whitechapel message board). Wow! Awesomeness beyond compare. Enjoy.

THE 2010 STEAMPUNK WORLD'S FAIR: A REASON TO VISIT NEW JERSEY

WEIRD TALES is proud to be a sponsor of the Steampunk World's Fair, the East Coast's first full-scale arts & music festival devoted to hybridizing far-out fantasy and science fiction with glorious Victorian-era extravagance! The excitement takes place May 14–16 at the Radisson Hotel in Piscataway, New Jersey. Attendees will enjoy a full schedule of musical performances and art exhibitions—and a Lovecraftian murder mystery!—and *Weird Tales* will be hosting the "Library of Lost Literature," featuring readngs by authors including Ellen Kushner (*The Privilege of the Sword*), Ben H. Winters (*Sense and Sensibility and Sea Monsters*), Ekaterina Sedia (*The Alchemy of Stone*), and many more. Plus: don't miss the fantastical poetry slam! For info: **www.steampunkworldsfair.com**.

The Bazaar

Salvaged Spirits

IN THE SHADOW OF THE MOUNTAIN, ONE MAN'S STRANGE STATUARY BRINGS FLOTSAM BACK TO LIFE

www.danielklennert.com

WE WERE DRIVING UP Washington State Route 706 to Mount Rainier, that Pacific Northwest mist hanging in the air just thick enough to throw everything into soft focus, when suddenly Stacy pressed her hand against the passenger side window and said, "What was *that?*" I turned just in

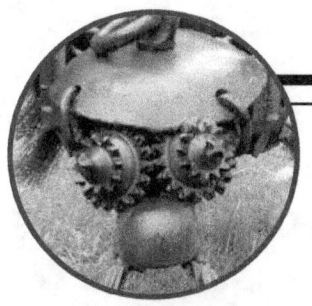

time to see what appeared to be a full-size giraffe . . . *skeleton* . . . standing in an open field next to a driveway framed by a huge iron gate. Hoping the open gate meant "Come in," we backed up and drove into the field—thus discovering Dan Klennert's *Ex Nihilo* sculpture park: four acres of larger-than-life beasts made from rusty iron and stout driftwood. A ten-foot-tall horse made of horseshoes, a metal death angel on a chopper, a giant 19th-century penny-farthing bike, a train locomotive the size of a minivan, a big mutant mechanical spider. It is a strange, anomalous oasis amid a national wilderness area; perhaps the Seattle/Portland steampunk scene (a la the likes of Cherie Priest, Lisa Mantchev, and Jay Lake, all found in this issue) permeates the regional consciousness. In any case, it is a weird piece of roadside culture worth visiting.
—*Stephen H. Segal*

CREEPY GOTH DOLLS
www.bastet2329.com
It's something of a relief to see the inherent creepiness of dolls made explicit, just as it would be a relief to see anyone acknowledge a terrible secret. Clearly, these little porcelain nightmares whisper their secrets to Christie, the artist who creates them; sad and beautiful, their preciousness maimed or made ghastly, they all have a story to tell. Christie takes a weird kind of pity on discarded dolls, rescuing them from junk shops and breaking them until they tell stories. They're scary, they're pitiful, they're haunting, and they are all adoptable at Christie's online shop.
—*Amanda Gannon*

WYRDING STUDIOS
www.wyrdingstudios.com
Wyrd: it means fate, destiny, the intersection of destiny with human will. Or, in the case of Wyrding Studios, the intersection of stone and silver, jewelry and fantasy. Kythryne Aisling coaxes unbelievable shapes out of strands of wire; her jewelry has a fairyland feel, ancient yet ageless, shining silver weaving a glamor around polished stone. Visitors to Wyrding Studios' online store can browse regularly  updated stock, commission custom pieces, or enroll in any of several monthly jewelry subscriptions. Kythryne also features "Intermittent Mysteries," past themes for which have included Arthurian myth, wanderlust, and all things oceanic. This wearable art will please any jewelry-loving magpie. —*A.G.*

The Library

Interview | BY JASON HELLER

A Better class of Criminal?

...NO. JESSE BULLINGTON EXPLAINS WHY HE DIGS THE GRAVEROBBERS OF 1364 A.D.

INTO THE CRACKS of history have fallen all kinds of minor, unheralded miscreants and dastards. In his debut novel, *The Sad Tale of the Brothers Grossbart,* Jesse Bullington has fabricated two such characters—the twin brothers Hegel and Manfriend Grossbart, graverobbers and, oddly enough, amateur philosophers—to poke holes in the social and theological fabric of Europe circa 1364. But there's more than simple historical fiction happening here: Willed into being by the worldview of a pre-scientific era, witches and demons and mermaids and pigs on two feet populate the periphery of Bullington's riotous, grotesquely picaresque adventure. At the center of the shit-storm stand the Brothers themselves—men of the hard streets before most streets were paved—who stagger and swagger on their quest for worldly rewards (and, in a weird kind of way, enlightenment). With a simple plot that exists mostly as a coat hanger for Bullington's teeming imagery, decadent prose, and whipcrack dialogue, the story zooms from satire to horror to theological banter in the twitch of an eye, with an overall effect that's as exhilarating as it is deliciously unsettling. It's mostly up to the reader to decide if the roguish Grossbarts are behind, ahead of, or simply out of their time. Much can be said of the book itself—although it's Bullington's irreverant, uncompromising take on both genre fiction and human nature that makes *The Brothers Grossbart* one of the most foully refreshing fantasies in ages.

Why 1364? I knew the general era I wanted the story to take place in, but I postponed fixing a set date until I hit on something historical I absolutely had to include. I was researching at the same time I was writing and found a historical event I wanted the Brothers to take part in that occurred in 1365. That settled it. I knew it would take a long time to get them from their starting point in the novel to where said event took place, however, so I pushed the first chapter back to late 1364. Once I fixed the date I had to rewrite a lot of what I had already written for accuracy, but to me that part of the process is a lot of (masochistic) fun.

Your treatment of the supernatural in *The Brothers Grossbart* verges on magic realism. Do you think it's an accurate representation of how Europeans saw their world back then?

The world was a much stranger, mysterious place in the late medieval era, and considering the content of period bestiaries I think that some Europeans certainly saw their world in a fashion similar to how I've portrayed them. On the other hand, primary sources I've come across imply there were at least a few skeptics and agnostics, even among the uneducated lower classes, so I wouldn't assume everyone in Europe was superstitious, let alone convinced of the corporality of witches

and monsters. Seeing is believing, of course.

There's a lot of subversion of fantasy tropes in the book—much of it juicily gruesome. What possessed you?

The spirit of Ronnie James Dio. No. I grew up on Tolkien and role-playing games and reading pulp fantasy, adventure and horror and watching cheesy movies of the same. But the older I got the more bored I grew with seeing the same things ad nauseam, so I decided to write a satire. With satire you're free to include as many hackneyed tropes and gags as you

THE SAD TALE OF THE BROTHERS GROSSBART by Jesse Bullington (Orbit, $14.99, paperback)

can cram in, so long as you carefully subvert them, with the result being the sort of weird send-up that both diehard genre fans and haters can get behind. I have an enormous amount of love for fantasy, but that doesn't mean I don't get a thrill out of seeing it get down and dirty.

As crass and nasty as the Grossbarts are, they're constantly waxing theological. They even have a moral code, mangled as it is. Was that equation a difficult one to balance?

Most crass and nasty people do think they're in the right, and they have their own internal codes which they operate under. I endeavored to write the Grossbarts as a psychic alien observer might, as opposed to one of their victims who only hears the external half of their dialogues and has the sort of prejudice against them that being clobbered with a shovel imparts. That sounded weird. But really, we all have elaborate and detailed personal belief systems that justify certain behaviors and actions, and so writing believable characters is simply a matter of remembering this and representing it even when the outlook of said fictitious characters is wildly at odds with what is common or acceptable.

It seems the book has already gained a reputation. Are you afraid it might get pigeonholed—even by those who like it—as being crude for crudeness' sake?

Any time you try doing something different you risk alienating certain readers—but that's no reason not to try something different. Obviously the novel has its crude qualities and individual scenes, but I think that aspect has been played up at the expense of other aspects, which is a shame. Furthermore, dismissing it as "crude for crudeness' sake" is rather missing the many points of writing such a graphic text—namely, emulating earlier works (Rabelais' Gargantua and Pantagruel, Cervantes' Don Quixote, and even some of the Romances, such as *The Romance of Reynard*); restoring a sense of realism long absent from fantasy and adventure epics; calling out overly-sanitized fiction, subverting the reader's expectations; etc. In the end, of course, worrying about whether or not strangers will appreciate my work as a nuanced satire or dismiss it as a gross-out opus is exactly the sort of thing that will water down my writing, so I try my best not to think about such things—at least until I get a nasty review to grumble over. ☺

NEO-VICTORIAN FUN

THE EQUIVOQUE PRINCIPLE by Darren Craske (HarperCollins, $12.95, paperback)
A travelling circus in Victorian London! The strongman accused of horrific murders! The magic-wielding circus owner on the case! Craske's prose is slapdash, but his scenarios and enthusiasm are infectious.

THE STRANGELY BEAUTIFUL TALE OF MISS PERCY PARKER by Leanna Renee Hieber (Leisure Books, $6.99, paperback)
A feminine counterpart to the masculine *Equivoque*, Hieber's debut novel gives us an unreconstructed gothic-romance heroine in Percy Parker, an oh-so-bright but

terribly timid albino girl of mysterious origins and spectral visions, whose enrollment in London's Athens Academy marks her entrance into a world of shadowy war between goddesses and devils. The man who knows the secrets is Professor Rychman, for whom Percy quivers with longing; much emo ensues, as does a surprisingly fresh take on Jack the Ripper.

SERVANTS OF THE SUPERNATURAL by Antonio Melechi (Arrow Books, $16.95, paperback)
Victorian folks sure did love their seances and mesmerism. University of York scholar Melechi takes us on a tour of the era's spiritualist obsession, from hypnotic medicine to communication with the afterlife.

EDISON'S CONCRETE PIANO by Judy Wearing (ECW Press, $17.95, paperback)
Lest we get so caught up in magic that we forget about the gears, Canadian science scholar Wearing collects sixteen true stories of bygone inventors and their most glorious failures: Leonardo da Vinci's walk-on-water shoes, Nikola Tesla's earthquake machine, Alexander Graham Bell's six-nippled sheep, and more.

CONVERSATIONS WITH THE WEIRD TALES CIRCLE edited by John Pelan & Jared Waters (Centipede Press, $225, hardcover)
The early days of *Weird Tales*, in the 1920s and '30s, marked a path out of Victorian fantasy into modernity. This lush, oversized, 754-page history digs up old letters and rare writings to share the lives not only of H.P. Lovecraft and Robert E. Howard but of less-remembered fantasy geniuses like C.L. Moore and Fritz Leiber. An expensive tome, but there's treasure within.

NEW AND FANTASTIC

THE HUNDRED THOUSAND KINGDOMS by N.K. Jemisin (Orbit, $13.99, paperback)
This remarkable debut novel is *not* steampunk, but its alchemic mix of epic fantasy, cosmic science fiction, royal court intrigue, and profound sensuality ought to excite fans of every spec-fic subgenre. The young barbarian noblewoman Yeine is summoned to the miraculous floating city-palace of Sky, where her grandfather reigns over the world and her decadent cousin toys dangerously with the enslaved god of chaos, Nahadoth. Politics mixes with sorcery as war looms; also, a *phenomenal* sex scene.

BOOK OF THE
CENTURY

BONESHAKER INTRODUCES A NEW WORLD
OF 19TH-CENTURY SCIENCE FANTASY:
CHERIE PRIEST'S 'CLOCKWORK CENTURY,'
WHERE THE CIVIL WAR BURNS IN THE SKIES
AND SEATTLE IS OVERRUN WITH ZOMBIES

PHOTO BY CAITLIN KITTREDGE

I T IS THE late 19th century; the Civil War has dragged on for decades, thus accelerating the pace of wartime technology; and up in the northwest territories, a mad inventor named Leviticus Blue has, while test-driving his nightmarishly gigantic earth-moving drill, accidentally unleashed a subterranean gas that turned the inhabitants of Seattle into zombies. Sixteen years later, Seattle has been encased within a protective wall to keep the horrors contained—but Blue's teenage son Zeke is determined to redeem his father's name, so he makes his way into the city to see what he can find. Now it's up to Zeke's mother, Briar Wilkes, to catch a lift over the walls on a smuggler's airship and drag his ass back out again before he gets himself killed.

That's the furiously unfolding scenario author Cherie Priest tosses us into with *Boneshaker*, her first grand adventure in a steampunk America she calls "The Clockwork Century." We asked Cherie, a *Weird Tales* contributor herself, to tell us more.

What came first, the chicken or the egg? Which is to say: *Boneshaker* is an awesome story set in an awesome milieu. Did the creation start with Leviticus Blue and his Drill? With a kid breaking into a walled city of zombies? Or with the world of a decades-long Civil War fueling advanced military weaponry?

Boneshaker started with the vague idea that I wanted to write a novel set in Seattle. I'd lived here a couple of years, and I was starting to feel like I had a handle on the city; and this collided with my pre-existing interest in steampunk— which is quite popular here. But then, once these two ideas had met, I had to

back away a bit. I wanted my steampunk/alternate-history universe to have a good grounding, and at least a hypothetical historic base for its odd tech.

So I got thinking about how war does so much to advance technology—and I went poking around through some of the old patents that were filed toward the end of the Civil War. With a little digging you can find specs and plans for amazing, epic battle machines of all makes and shapes, but these machines never happened because the inventors ran out of war. That's where I got the idea to extend The Late Unpleasantness, so that America's late Victorian period would be advanced in some strange, bleak ways.

BONESHAKER by Cherie Priest
(Tor, $15.99, paperback)
www.clockworkcentury.com

Naturally, I then had to back fill a scenario wherein the war might have gone on for so long; but speculating on alternate war outcomes is practically the regional pastime of the southeast—and I'm a southern girl at heart. It didn't take me long to put some things together, and then—once I finally had my warped American 19th century—I was free to consider Seattle and the oddball things I could set here.

I suppose that sounds weird, considering how little impact the Civil War had on the Pacific Northwest, but there you go. Once I had my national background, and once I'd figured out how to "destroy" the city . . . everything just fell into place.

Briar Wilkes is one tough cookie—both in her grim workaday life to support her son, and in full-on heroic mode to rescue him from Seattle. Can you talk a little about her character and how she came to be? I can't think of many teen-flavored adventure books that star the teenager's mom as the main hero. Are there real people, either loved ones or historical figures, buried in Briar's genetics?

Briar is an unabashed homage to Sarah Connor and Ellen Ripley, for starters. And beyond that, I wanted to put a woman my own age in an adventure story. There's so much fiction out there featuring very young women—and they're so often presented as righteous badasses who behave like they have the life experience of someone much older. But my own favorite female heroines are the two aforementioned—neither of whom are improbably young, and both of whom end up in ferocious mother-bear situations where they pull out all the stops to survive and protect their charges.

I've seen critics talk about how it's a cheap trick, putting a woman's child in danger—that it's an obvious ploy, and it can unfavorably pigeonhole women in fiction. But I don't think that's fair. There's an intense, primal power inherent in motherhood and/or the protective instinct. Why would you disparage or ignore that? Obviously there are other great stories to tell about women, absolutely—but let's not throw out the baby with the bathwater.

I love the fact that, though *Boneshaker* is set in an American city rather than in a magical fantasy world, the book opens with a map. How much does geography affect your storytelling—in this book, and in gen-

"Briar Wilkes is an unabashed homage to Sarah Connor and Ellen Ripley, for starters. And beyond that, I wanted to put a woman my own age into an adventure story."

eral? Should more stories of all kinds come with maps?

Well, all the running around in *Boneshaker* does get a bit confusing after awhile; so with that in mind, my editor proposed a map and I was all over it. I went down to the Seattle Public Library and hit up their special collections department, where I found a map that was roughly contemporary to the story. I took pictures of it and sent them back to Tor, spent some time with Photoshop marking key locations . . . and then a wonderful artist came along and did the rest. I'm excessively pleased with the result; I think it looks fabulous!

But the geography of Seattle is a little strange, especially if you're talking about the city's early years and adding a wall around it. Right around the turn of the 20th century (or shortly after it), there was this giant terra-forming project best known as the "Denny Regrade." (In short, the city tore down a huge hill that overlooked part of the downtown area. It was an enormous undertaking and it changed the shape of the city forever.) And likewise, the city spent about a dozen years lifting the old quarter off the mud flats—raising the street levels as much as thirty feet.

So particularly before these regrades, Seattle came custom-made with a bit of a crowded, jumbled feel; and I think that the map was genuinely helpful to people who might have a hard time following the action. But the truth is, I like maps anyway. I'd be delighted to see more maps in more books, whether or not they are strictly utilitarian.

Hey, why do people love airships so much, anyway? For that matter, why do they love zombies so damn much?

What's not to love about airships? They fly, they look cool, and they come with pirates. As for zombies, well, they're just plain awesome. They're group-oriented; they're good listeners; they aren't materialistic; and they love you for your brains.

***Boneshaker* is a story of hope amid hopelessness. Are you an optimist or a pessimist? Why?**

Depends on my mood. Well, here in Seattle, it often depends on the weather. I get some pretty epic seasonal-affective issues here.

But to answer your question, I'm probably an optimist—at least from a narrative standpoint. I get bored/frustrated with stories that are all woe and no redemption—for example, I don't care for horror stories wherein every-single-body dies at the end. I'm good with some hardcore grimness, sure; but someone needs to get out alive. Someone has to conquer. Along those same lines, when I see a movie or read a book and none of the characters learns anything, or if everything stays exactly the same . . . I mean, why did I bother? I could've just stayed home and watched cartoons. I find it much more interesting when people claw their way through impossible circumstances to stand bedraggled and triumphant on the top of the heap. ☉

The second book in **Cherie Priest**'s Clockwork Century series, *Dreadnought*, will be published by Tor Books in 2010, and a novelette set in the same world, "Tanglefoot," will appear this year both at *Subterranean Online* and in Ann & Jeff VanderMeer's *Steampunk Reloaded* anthology. Priest's previous novels include *Fathom*, *Four and Twenty Blackbirds*, *Wings to the Kingdom*, and *Not Flesh Nor Feathers*; she contributed an essay on Poe to the fall 2009 issue of *Weird Tales*. More info: www.cheriepriest.com

Steampunk Classics

THE
ANGEL
OF THE
REVOLUTION

THE THRILLING 1893 AIRSHIP ROMANCE

George Griffith

THE SECRET MECHANICAL

Man

BOILERPLATE! THE ROBOT WHO AMAZED THE 1893 WORLD FAIR! IN OUR EXCLUSIVE INTRODUCTION TO THIS EXCERPT FROM THEIR NEW BOOK, **PAUL GUINAN AND ANINA BENNETT** EXPLAIN WHY YOU'RE JUST NOW HEARING ABOUT THIS MARVELOUS METAL SOLDIER....

"HISTORY IS WRITTEN by the winners," George Orwell observed in 1944. Even at the time, that maxim had been floating around for so long that no one remembers who coined it.

Then there's this cheery comment, from Napoleon Bonaparte: "History is a set of lies that people have agreed upon."

And this, courtesy of the man immortalized as Lawrence of Arabia: "The documents are liars. No man ever yet tried to write down the entire truth of any action in which he has been engaged."

History is, in fact, littered with pithy remarks about how utterly subjective and unreliable human accounts of historic events are. So why bother pouring years of effort into a lavishly illustrated history book that further muddies the waters by plopping a steampunk robot, of all things, into the flow of real events?

The short answer is that everyone loves robots.

BOILERPLATE by Paul Guinan and Anina Bennett (Abrams, $24.95, hardcover) www.bigredhair.com

Some reviewers have called *Boilerplate: History's Mechanical Marvel* an "alternate history" about a robot who has adventures with famous historical figures such as Teddy Roosevelt and the aforementioned T.E. Lawrence. My husband and co-author, Paul Guinan, and I think of it as a real history book . . . plus one robot. And we think history is always worth exploring—because the acts of thinking, writing, and talking about history are among humanity's best shots at understanding ourselves. (Not to mention the fact that history is full of ripping good yarns.)

Paul, a self-proclaimed "huge history buff," originally created Boilerplate for a graphic novel that was never published. "I'm always looking for ways to dramatize history," he says. But in the 1990s, when there were fewer publishers and fewer genres in the graphic novel arena, it was tough to find a home for the "straight" history tales he wanted to tell.

Taking a cue from his favorite author, Gore Vidal, Paul decided to try bringing history alive through a fictional protagonist. He picked the period that most fascinated him—the turn of the 19th/20th century—added a robot, and thus was born Boilerplate.

From the start, Paul planned to do a photo essay as a backup feature in the graphic novel, presented as if the story were based on a real 19th-century robot. He built an articulated figurine from scratch and started Photoshopping it into historical images. It struck him that this approach would be a great way to tell true stories from the past. Then the graphic novel was killed in midstream. But by that time, Boilerplate had a hold on Paul. In July 2000, he started posting his Boilerplate photos with short stories on our web site (www.BoilerplateRobot.com), with my editorial help. To this day, he gets email from people who believe that a bipedal, talking, possibly sentient robot actually existed in 1893. Which goes to show that common sense isn't as common as one might hope.

Other, more discerning readers quickly fell under Boilerplate's spell too. Over the next few years, the robot developed a cult following and garnered international press. In one interview, Paul off-handedly mentioned that he wanted to do a Boilerplate coffee-table book. Lo and behold, a publisher who read the article contacted him and made an offer!

Paul recruited me to write most of the new material while he focused on the book's hundreds of historical images. This wasn't just a matter of adapting the existing Boilerplate stories into book format; the book is vastly expanded beyond our web site. The text is peppered with quotations that, like the images, are a mixture of real history, mostly real history, and made-up history. We locked ourselves inside our house and worked feverishly for months.

Then, mere weeks before our deadline for the final manuscript, our publisher went out of business. Paul and I wondered if the robot was cursed. With the book so close to completion, though, we couldn't succumb to superstition. Finally we signed up with a literary agent, who immediately piqued the interest of several bigger publishers. We wound up with a beautiful hardcover book published by Abrams in October 2009, and we've already started on a companion book.

Boilerplate: History's Mechanical Marvel is a tour of selected events from world history, circa 1870-1920, with the robot and its inventor, Archibald Campion, as guides. Please be our guests for the next seven pages as we follow their excursion through the World's Columbian Exposition of 1893—the site of Boilerplate's unveiling, and of so many other marvels of 19th-century technology. . . .

WONDER OF THE WHITE CITY

—— or ——

THE MECHANICAL MAN MEETS THE PUBLIC

Archibald Campion was true to his word.
In summer 1893, he revealed his latest creation:
a walking, talking mechanical man. A robot.

A local newspaper takes pride in
Chicago's rise from the ashes of the
Great Conflagration to become a
world-class urban center and host of
the pinnacle of cultural achievement:
an international exposition.

"UNFOLDED GENIUS"

Archie introduced Professor Campion's Mechanical Marvel—
which didn't come to be known as *Boilerplate* until years
later—at the World's Columbian Exposition, an ambitious
world's fair held in Chicago.

The World's Columbian Exposition occupies a crucial
juncture in U.S. history. It both reflected and shaped our
nation's evolution, symbolizing as well as spurring the transi-
tion from agricultural to industrial, rural to urban, producer
to consumer society. For Americans and Chicagoans alike,
the 1893 World's Fair embodied aspirations to be seen in
a new light, to play a more sophisticated role. For Archie
Campion, it was the beginning of a new chapter in his life.

*"So accustomed had I grown to working day in and day
out, utterly absorbed in constructing my mechanical soldier,
that upon its completion I felt at first a sense of great relief and
accomplishment, followed at once by panic. Having created this*

"**MAKE NO LITTLE
PLANS; THEY HAVE
NO MAGIC TO STIR
MEN'S BLOOD.**"
—Daniel H. Burnham,
Director of Works,
Columbian Exposition

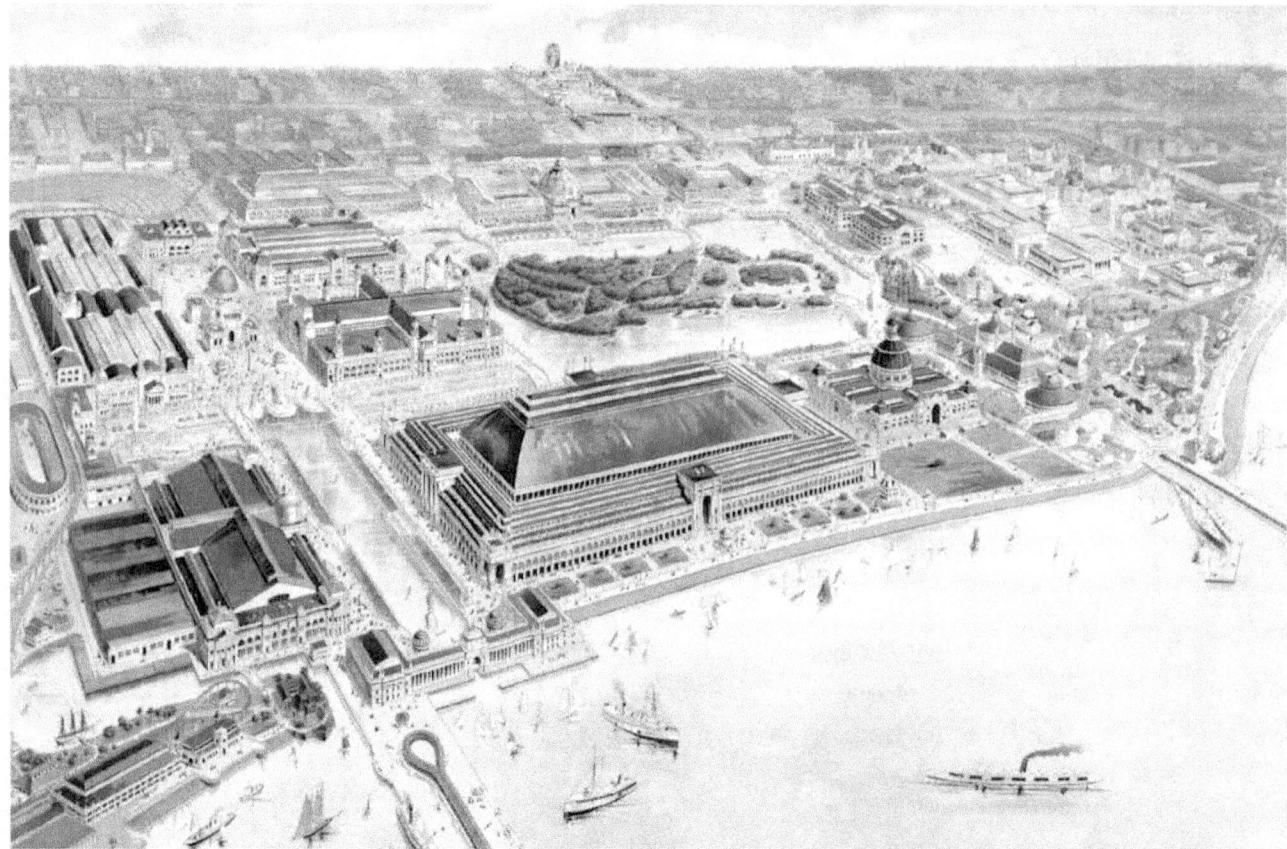

marvel, I now face the far more onerous chore of peddling it like a street vendor!"

—Archibald Campion, letter to Mark Twain (May 1, 1893)

Archie was granted a space in Machinery Hall, one of the fourteen Great Buildings that housed most of the fair's 65,000 exhibits. Artfully landscaped canals, lagoons, and causeways connected these classically styled white edifices into an idealized, orderly *White City*. Electric boats plied the waters, powered by Edward Fullerton's fuel cells.

Inside Machinery Hall, Archie's exhibit was dwarfed by endless rows of state-of-the-art mechanical devices and tools, with special attractions such as Eli Whitney's cotton gin, the world's largest conveyor belt, and a cutting-edge power plant that generated electricity for the whole fair. At night the fairgrounds were illuminated by electric lights, thanks to an early alternating-current system developed by Archie's friend Nikola Tesla. The world had never seen anything like it.

"In the mammoth corridors of Machinery Hall at the World's Fair the zenith of nine-teenth century progress in the mechanical arts was reached, and the artisans of every civilized clime learned something of practical benefit from the unfolded genius of the world's greatest inventors. Perhaps most highly regarded by fellow inventors was Professor Campion's remarkable anthropomorphic machine, which imagination allows could be of varied benefit to mankind."

—Henry Davenport Northrop, *Pictorial History of the World's Fair* (Union Publishing House, 1893)

THE SOUNDS OF PROGRESS

Boilerplate's unveiling on May 23, 1893, less than two weeks after the fair opened, was a bit anticlimactic. Archie demonstrated the robot in front of a modest crowd, eliciting a few gasps.

"Cam and I visited Machinery Hall today... you recall how he does like to know about every newfangled thingamajig under the sun. Well, for once even he was confounded. There was this fellow called Champion, showing a kind of metal soldier. A big iron man.

It took two years and $25 million to transform 630 acres of swampy Chicago lakeshore into the neoclassical fantasyland of the 1893 World's Columbian Exposition. The guiding lights were Frederick Law Olmsted, who designed Central Park in Manhattan, and Daniel Burnham, who became a major force in architecture and urban planning. Burnham oversaw all the construction, paying particular attention to the fair's fourteen Great Buildings, which collectively boasted 63 million square feet of floor space.

Originally intended to celebrate the 400th anniversary of Columbus's 1492 landing in North America, the fair was a bit late—but no one seemed to mind. It attracted around 27 million visitors, at a time when the population of the entire United States was only about 63 million. People even paid to gawk while it was under construction.

PROFESSOR CAMPION'S
MECHANICAL MARVEL

⬆ A rare interior view of Machinery Hall. Boilerplate peers down on Archie Campion's booth from the balcony. Some of the exhibit halls inside the Great Buildings, although copiously described in writing by various authors, were not well documented photographically.

➡ A souvenir postcard of Machinery Hall, one of the fair's fourteen Great Buildings and the site of Boilerplate's unveiling.

PROFESSOR CAMPION AND HIS METAL MANSERVANT

DANCING GIRL
STREET
OF CAIRO.

"I tell you what, that contraption walked and talked all on its own! It lifted up two grown men over its head as if they was feathers. It saluted and marched about and aimed a rifle like a real soldier. They showed how it couldn't be hurt. At the end it looked square at me, bowed just as proper as you please, and said 'Good day ma-dam. Did you en-joy the de-mon-stra-tion?' 'I surely did' says I 'but I don't know why I'm telling that to a machine!' To which it says 'Be-cause I asked.'"

—Jolene Gibson, letter to Susan Gibson (May 23, 1893)

Archie gave a short speech about the robot's intended purpose, which the audience greeted with polite applause before moving along to the next attraction. Due to the overwhelming noise from the multitude of machines being demonstrated in Machinery Hall, most spectators probably couldn't even hear what Archie had said.

From the roof of the Manufactures and Liberal Arts Building, Boilerplate, Lily Campion, and a couple of Columbian Guards gaze southeast across the White City. Machinery Hall, where Boilerplate made its public debut, can be seen at upper right.

"I did not anticipate, and you may not be aware of, the deafening array of sounds emitted by the mechanical exhibits in Machinery Hall. This fact is conspicuously omitted from the many guidebooks, magazines, and pamphlets devoted to the Columbian Exposition. Imagine a single cavernous room, surpassing 435,000 square feet in floor area, filled with the unceasing din of banging, clanging, clattering, sparking, sputtering, squealing, hissing, and occasionally explosive devices, and you may have some inkling of what we endure. I am thankful that my aural capacity and Lily's do not seem to have suffered any ill effect."

—Archibald Campion, letter to Frank Reade Jr. (May 26, 1893)

Archie Campion tours the Midway Plaisance with his sister, Lily. She is being pushed along by Boilerplate in a rolling chair, a convenience available for rent at the fair (75 cents per hour or six dollars per day). The multiculturalism of the world's first Midway was a rarity in 1893. It was so full of strange sights that Boilerplate barely got a second glance from the crowds of curiosity seekers, most of whom were more interested in the Egyptian belly dancers.

➡ Boilerplate with its original military kit, which the robot wore during the Spanish-American War. At Winston Churchill's urging, the shoulder pouch and helmet designs were later adapted as part of the British Army's official field uniform.

⬅ Sketch artists experienced a surge in demand from a variety of magazines and special publications that commissioned illustrations to give their readers an inside view of the World's Columbian Exposition.

BAD TIMING

Although some of Archie's colleagues recognized the promise of the technology behind Boilerplate, the robot wasn't exactly an overnight sensation. On top of the noise problem in Machinery Hall, Archie was plagued by timing problems. For starters, the date he picked to unveil Boilerplate was the same day Thomas Edison chose to demonstrate the much-hyped *kinetoscope*, the forerunner of modern movie projectors, in the Electricity Building. It was most people's first chance to see the kinetoscope in action, and there was no resisting the siren call of a new form of entertainment.

Unlike most other exhibits, Boilerplate wasn't confined to its exhibit hall. Archie and Lily took the robot with them whenever they explored the fair. Their excursions generated enough public excitement that Archie

(cont. on page 28)

A souvenir spoon from the 1893
world's fair. Embossed on the handle
is an image of Boilerplate's head,
and on the bowl is Machinery Hall.

This embroidered ribbon,
handed out at the fair as a
souvenir in Machinery Hall,
is now a rare collectible.

decided to invite the press to a pre-scheduled Boilerplate publicity tour of the fairgrounds.

But that went awry, too: They were upstaged by the Infanta (Princess) Eulalia of Spain, the youngest daughter of Queen Isabella II. Eulalia, visiting as an official representative of her country, was greeted with much pomp and circumstance. Royalty had become chic again in the United States, and all eyes were on the Infanta wherever she went. Boilerplate garnered only a smattering of press coverage, mainly as a curiosity.

"It was my fine fortune to be present when the mechanical man and its inventor perambulated the Fair grounds. Everywhere, they were the objects of astonished glances, exclamations of wonder, and the occasional shriek from a timid soul. I scarcely believed my own ears when the automaton uttered a direct reply to my query about its activities: 'I will ride in the Ferris Wheel.' That leg of its tour attracted a considerable number of onlookers, all of whom were, alas, entirely excluded from hobnobbing with the machine-man owing to its being so heavy as to require a private car on the great Wheel."

—Nicholas Stanley Parker,
"The Walking Mechanical Miracle of the World's Fair," *World's Columbian Exposition Extra* (June 1893)

Boilerplate was not, in fact, heavy enough to warrant its own car on the Ferris Wheel. Each car was the size of a bus and could hold sixty people. A more likely explanation is that the robot's weight was used as an excuse, in order to avoid any disputes over who would get to ride in the same car with it.

Even Archie's announced purpose for Boilerplate, as a prototype soldier *"for use in resolving the conflicts of nations,"* wasn't particularly well timed. Despite growing social unrest and economic disparity within its borders, the U.S. was officially at peace with other nations in 1893.

Most people had never heard of the 1871 Korean War, and of course no one yet knew that in only five years the United States would invade Cuba and the Philippines during the Spanish-American War. Or that the next century would bring two unthinkable world wars. The idea of a mechanical soldier was easily shrugged off as fanciful and unnecessary.

INFORMATION OVERLOAD

In retrospect, it's hard to understand how such an advanced, groundbreaking invention as Boilerplate could have gotten lost in the shuffle. But at the time, there were so many special events and celebrities, so many novelties and exotic cultures being introduced to a dazzled public, that a man-size automaton seemed only mildly remarkable. There was too much competition.

The fair showcased *"every device that genius could suggest and money supply,"* in the words of Bertha Honoré Palmer, who headed the Board of Lady Managers. Exhibitors from around the globe brought with them all manner of inventions, materials, goods, arts, foodstuffs, machinery, ideas, publications, crafts, games, and customs. Back then, it was the closest thing to a collective, interactive knowledge base like the Internet—but in physical form, all in one place, and temporary.

To average fairgoers, Boilerplate was certainly a sight to see, yet merely one of countless clever innovations. Many people were delighted in equal measure by the robot, the world's first Ferris Wheel, and the convenient new hot cereal mix called *Cream of Wheat*.

"The World's Fair of 1893 was an astounding, bewildering assemblage of art and industry, all the more so for a young lad still in short pants. Matthew recalls: 'I saw so many wonderful

The Tin Man undergoes repair. William Wallace Denslow, the original Oz artist, patterned the look of the Tin Man after Boilerplate at Baum's request.

things that I hardly knew what I liked most, and it all is so confused in my mind that I hardly know now what I did see.

"Two things I recollect of note, one being my first glimpse of an electrified city at night, the Court of Honor lighted as though by stars come down from the heavens. The other being the brief terror of accidental parting from my parents, then the thrill of getting whisked up by Professor Campion's metal man, what found my family and reunited us. How my brother was the picture of envy! He tried to keep me from viewing the Monster Cheese in the Agricultural Building, but Mum and Dad wouldn't have none of his fuss.'"

—Edith Aldrich, interview with Matthew McKeough, *Memories of the White City* (Pericles Press, 1909)

SHADOW ON THE WHITE CITY

Boilerplate and other lesser-known exhibits were also overshadowed in the public mind by a series of tragedies surrounding the World's Columbian Exposition, including several fires, a smallpox epidemic, and the assassination of Chicago's Mayor Carter Harrison the day before the fair closed.

"Poor Archie. He certainly had not expected instantaneous success, nor was personal notoriety his objective. He desired only to spread word of his invention and foster interest in its potential military and commercial applications. The obstacles fate has thus far placed in his path are comically multitudinous. The fair, it seems, was precisely the wrong venue for the debut of his automatic soldier. We have discovered a new irony of the modern age: In a place where every thing is a wonderment, nothing is a wonderment."

—Lily Campion, letter to Paula Vincent (November 27, 1893)

Archie and Lily persevered, hatching a plan to show off Boilerplate's strength and versatility on an expedition to the South Pole. But while they laid their plans, Boilerplate would be drawn into its first armed conflict—on the streets of Chicago. ✪

LOVE, MUST

BY KURT KIRCHMEIER

illustration by Ming Doyle

IN WHICH A
MECHANI-BEAST HAS
SOMETHING IN COMMON
WITH ITS FLESHIER
COUNTERPARTS

HIDDEN WHEELS TURNED. Gears engaged. The elephant reared back and raised its leather-wrapped trunk to shower the rafters with clouds of hot steam—this while vibrating the walls and the floorboards with the stentorian sound that had earned the mechanical marvel its name: Trumpeter.

Julian smiled like a proud father, but his joy was short lived, quickly replaced by sadness. His precious elephant would soon be gone.

The man who had commissioned the work, one Viktor Krane, applauded the demonstration. "Wonderful," he declared, "just wonderful. A fine bit of invention. Very fine, indeed." His spectacles were small and his moustache well trimmed. He wore a suit of the finest wool.

Julian accepted the praise with the most fractional of nods. He'd never been comfortable with compliments.

The elephant, silent now within its stall, stood an impressive eight feet at the shoulder, its huge ears moving in such a way as to give one the impression the animal was fanning itself to remain cool. Its hide was suitably dry and cracked and its tusks were authentic ivory, threaded into copper fittings.

"Well, then," Viktor went on, "shall we attend to the unfortunate business of debts incurred? I trust your initial estimation did not prove egregiously low?"

If anything, "egregiously low" was an understatement, but then again, any sum would seem insufficient at this point.

Once again, Julian had allowed himself to grow attached to his work. And the elephant, for its part, wasn't making it any easier to let go; there was a rheumy quality about the animal's glass eyes that lent it an air of sad awareness, both of self and situation. Julian had tweaked the tear-pumps to remedy this, but his adjustments had failed to have the desired effect; it was as if the clockwork wonder truly was sad.

Julian cleared his throat. "Not egregiously, no," he said. "If you'll pardon me while I double-check my figures . . . "

The two of them were in Julian's stable-turned-workshop, surrounded by tables and shelves laden with various mechanical curiosities, not the least of which were a small grey mouse and a smaller copper toad. The former was repeatedly scurrying the length of a countertop, the latter continually leaping to avoid a collision.

Julian had set the rodent in motion so as to distract his prize pachyderm (elephants were said to be skittish around mice) from the conversation. An unnecessary bit of foolishness, he allowed, for surely the grey monstrosity possessed no grasp of human language, but still . . .

Julian consulted his ledger and added twenty-percent. He felt his heart grow abruptly heavy as he quoted the sum aloud, for to name a number was to make it official.

"Fair enough," said Viktor without hesitation. "If you would be so kind as to prepare the item for transport, I shall return at first light to retrieve it." He tipped an imaginary hat and bid Julian "Good day."

"Good day," Julian replied long after his buyer had exited the workshop.

The item, Viktor had said, as if it were a shovel or a saddle rather than a masterpiece of motion and sound. Ten months, he'd been working on Trumpeter, ten months of meticulous planning and careful assembly, of early mornings and extended evenings, obsessing over every detail.

Item, indeed. To Viktor Krane, the elephant was just one more oddity to add to an already legendary curio collection. Julian shook his head and regarded his crowning achievement. Trumpeter was different than all of the others; the design was much more ambitious, much more complex. Additional hours had strengthened the bond.

The elephant swished its tail, glossy eyes still fixed on the squeaky mouse.

You should be mine, Julian thought with a sigh, mine to keep.

But there was nothing for it. Ten months was a long time to subsist without pay; his cupboards were bare and his debts were high. He needed Viktor's money. He needed it desperately. And besides, the elephant had been commissioned; by rights, it belonged to another.

AS PER HIS word, Viktor returned at dawn.

Julian hadn't slept a wink. Instead, he'd spent the night pacing and pondering a way in which he might back out of the deal without running the risk of going hungry or alienating his wealthiest client.

But in the end, and in light of promises rendered, he was forced to resign himself to the harsh reality of the situation. And so just prior to sunrise he suspended his brainstorming in favor of spending what little time he had left with the result of nearly a year's devotion.

He stood at the elephant's side and rubbed its wonderfully floppy ears for what he suspected would be the very last time. Then he muttered a simple farewell and reached out for a lever marked: sleep emulation. He couldn't be sure, but in the seconds it took for those expressive eyes to close against the cruel, cruel world, Julian swore he heard the faintest whimper.

Strange, he thought afterwards; had he not cared so much, had he not invested his heart in every stitch and every gear, in every tiny lever and spinning wheel, he would never have accomplished such a grand feat and, consequently, would never have made the sale. Had he not cared so much, he would never have had to say goodbye.

If you love something, went an old proverb, let it go; it will find its way back to you if it was meant to be.

But Julian had to wonder at the teeth of this old saw; his recipe for success, after all, was exactly that: to love things and let them go.

"Might I inquire as to the nature of your next project?" asked Viktor. "Or will that jinx it? I know how superstitious you artisans can be." He chuckled, a phoney sound, honed for the false intimacies of a commercial climate, which was probably the only climate Viktor had ever known.

The same could likely have been said for Viktor's father and his father before him. Julian found he had no trouble at all imagining a family tree whose many branches supported similarly shallow men. Men of the sort who believed there existed nothing in life that couldn't be had for a price.

Julian shook his head. "I haven't decided yet," he said honestly.

"But you will send word of it, of course."

"Of course," said Julian. His voice sounded wooden even to his own ears.

The two men shook hands and Viktor departed, his purse unburdened and his trailer heavy with the weight of a clockwork obsession and the heart of a simple man, who stood looking on long after the caravan had disappeared into the distance.

* * *

JULIAN DUTIFULLY PAID down his debts and at long last filled up his pantry, but afterwards couldn't bring himself to lift his tools. It scarcely seemed worth the commitment now, the heartache.

His father had brought him up to believe that a man only got out of a thing what he was willing to put into it, and yet for all that Julian put into his works, the best he could ever hope for in return was money, and never enough to last him indefinitely, never enough to allow him to build with the intention of keeping.

Having already lived the life of a husband and father (his wife had passed unexpectedly the year before; their son now traveled the world to spread the word of God), Julian desired only to chase a dream long set aside in the name of familial responsibility, to devote himself entirely to miracles such as Trumpeter, a family born of copper and sweat.

Perhaps one day they'd put on a show, the clockwork menagerie working together in a way that flesh-and-blood animals never could. Julian imagined smiling parents paying admission, willful children wanting pets.

A pipe dream, he realized now, painful though it was to admit.

But nonetheless, he knew he could only resist for so long. At some point he'd return to his inventions; the only question that remained was whether he'd resign himself to humble pieces that required nothing in the way of personal sacrifice and offered nothing in the way of fulfillment, or set even loftier goals and suffer deeper sorrows because of it. He was damned if he did and damned if he didn't. Or so it seemed.

On day six of his doldrums, a letter arrived. It was from Viktor, and concerned an unexplained "malfunction." I request your immediate presence, the letter said.

And so Julian packed his bags and bought passage on a fast-moving carriage.

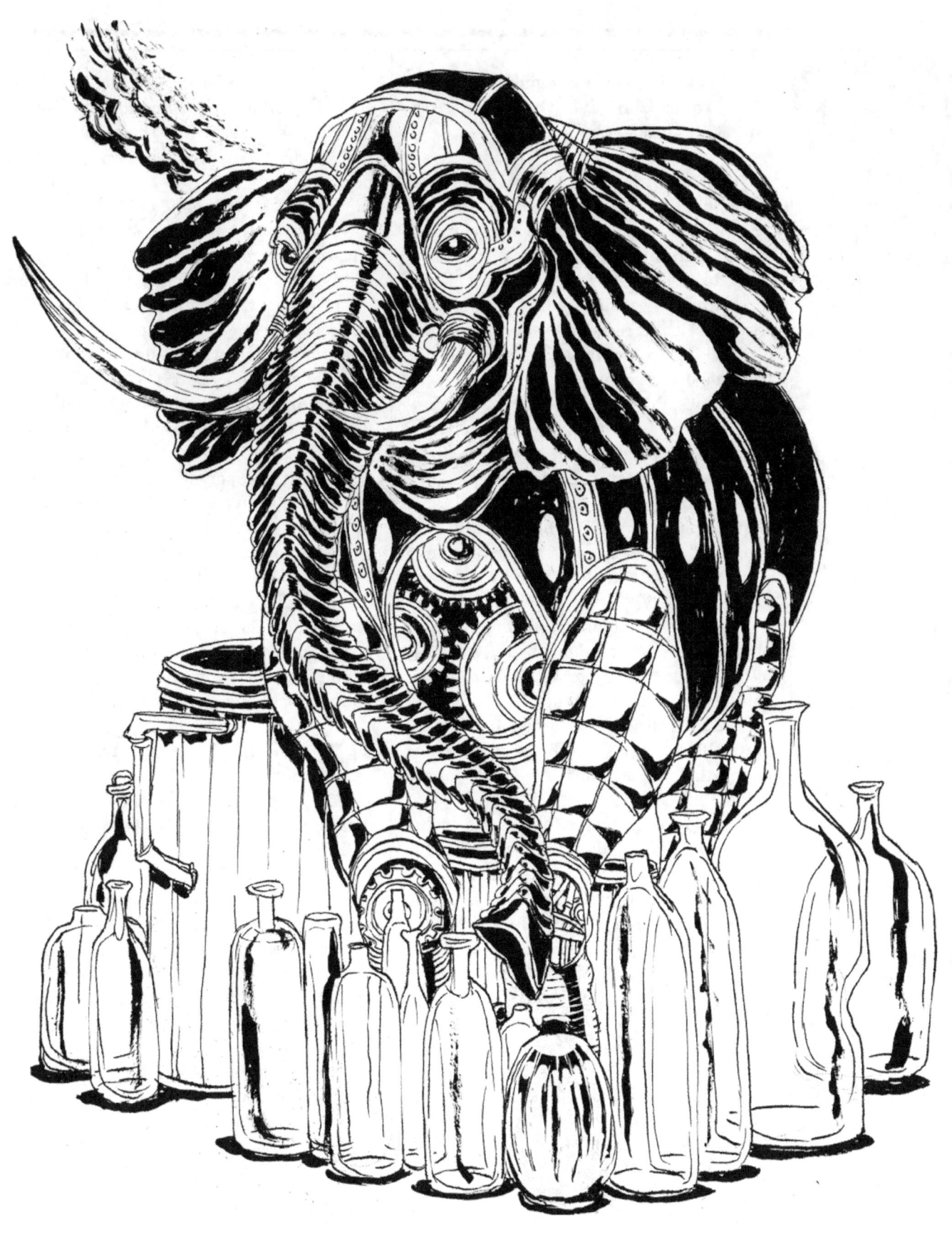

He was torn between excitement and guilt. Would those expressive eyes reveal recognition? Resentment?

THE ELEPHANT ROLLED its glass eyes wildly and raked the chill autumn air with ivory tusks, all the while trumpeting and straining against thick chains secured to an English Oak. Hot steam issued forth from the mad animal's trunk as it threw itself side to side; its ears flapped violently. Severe swelling could be seen in the temporal regions.

"Impossible," said Julian. It was currently the only word in his vocabulary.

"Well?" asked Viktor. "What in God's name is the matter with the brute?"

Julian shook his head. He had half a mind to pinch himself, so strange and surreal was the moment. "I honestly can't say," he replied, "but—"

"But what?" Viktor asked impatiently.

"Well," said Julian, "It's going to sound a little strange, but judging by the swelling of the . . . um . . . temporal glands, the poor thing appears to be in must."

Viktor raised an eyebrow, and understandably so, for as well he knew, the mechanical elephant didn't have any glands. "Must?" he asked.

"It's a sexually aggressive period exclusive to males," Julian explained. Trumpeter had apparently been raging for days, though how and under whose power, Julian couldn't begin to even guess.

"Are you telling me that this . . . this machine is a male?" Viktor Krane was beginning to show a harder edge.

Julian swallowed. "It seems so," he said, "though I assure you it's not of my doing."

"Well I should hope not," said Viktor, "because if I were to discover that this was some sort of clever ploy to get me to pay an extraordinary repair bill . . ."

"No charge," Julian promised. "On my word, not a penny."

Viktor eyed him skeptically, then straightened his collar and took a calming breath. "Well and good, then," he continued. "So I can trust you'll put an end to this nonsense?"

Trumpeter trumpeted as if in defiance, the rattling of the chain all but drowning out Julian's noncommittal reply. "I'll certainly do what I can," he said, though he wasn't sure it would amount to much. After all, how does one terminate must in an animal that, by rights, shouldn't even be capable of experiencing it?

Viktor left him to his unenviable task with the promise that he'd return in a few hours.

But it happened that a few hours might just as well have been a few minutes. Try as he might, Julian could not get close enough to carry out a simple inspection, much less a remedial adjustment.

Though clearly perturbed, Viktor maintained the composure of a gracious host and put Julian up in the guesthouse in the hope that tomorrow might prove a more fruitful day.

"PLEASE," SAID JULIAN. "Just calm down."

He'd approached the animal in as disarming a manner as he was capable, and still the brute showed no sign of letting up. A cautious step forward had prompted a trunk swing that missed his skull only narrowly. Steam continued to billow. The chains kept rattling. The elephant was loud.

Julian had read that the temporal swelling suffered by bulls in must caused significant pressure on the eyes, which in turn caused an excruciating pain not unlike that brought on by an abscessed tooth. Indeed, Trumpeter seemed to be experiencing exactly this sort of pain, ludicrous as the diagnosis sounded. The swelling had worsened overnight, and the temporal ducts were now leaking a fluid that looked to be equal parts oil and water.

What this new symptom indicated wasn't clear, but at the very least it was something to follow up on. Julian waited until the dripping fluid formed a modest puddle on the grass before risking a quick reach in to procure a sample on the tip of his finger.

An olfactory examination ruled out water and oil. The substance was heady and sweet, a cross between burnt sugar and musk. More cologne than bodily discharge, Julian thought as he filled a vial for later analysis. A man of Viktor's resources, he surmised, would have no trouble at all recruiting a scientist for such a study.

"And then perhaps we'll get to the bottom of things," he said to the stubborn elephant.

It happened that Viktor had just sat down for lunch when Julian arrived; he invited Julian to join him. It was only the two of them on a terrace overlooking an expansive tiered garden, and yet there was food enough for seven or more. The evidence of excess was decidedly off-putting.

The serving girl, on the other hand, was young and pert and rather enchanting. And a tad on the strange side as well, Julian thought. Her breathing seemed to grow heavier with her every trip to the table, and she was blushing and smiling in a way that bespoke of arousal.

Curiously, her mischievous smiles were aimed at none other than Julian himself. He noticed her sniffing the air when she refilled his teacup, and noticed also the erect nipples visible through the fabric of her top. He swallowed hard.

Viktor, perceptive man that he was, noticed as well. He shook his head. "First the elephant, and now my staff. What's come over you, Marissa? You're not yourself today."

"My apologies, milord," she said, "Must be something in the air." She winked at Julian and left the room.

Viktor watched her go, then belatedly caught a whiff of something himself.

"Hmm," he said, his nostrils tracking the mystery, "it is in the air, isn't it?" He narrowed his eyes at his guest. "Tell me, Julian, what is that scent you're wearing, and why does it effect young Marissa so?"

Julian hadn't the opportunity to mention the temporal secretions yet; the vial was still in his pocket. He opened his mouth with the intention of replying honestly, but then closed it as a sudden idea sprang to mind. "It's just something I've been working on," he lied. "Essential oils and alcohol."

Viktor raised an eyebrow. "Perfume?"

Julian nodded. "I must have gotten some on my hands."

"You surprise me," said Viktor. "I hadn't realized your genius extended beyond metalwork." And then he tilted his head in such a way that it became obvious his thoughts had turned mercantile. "Marissa!" he said, beckoning the girl back into the room.

She arrived momentarily. "Yes, milord?"

Viktor turned his gaze on Julian. "What say we test the scent in earnest, shall we?"

Julian shrugged and raised his hands, at which point Viktor asked the girl politely to humor two old men. She did as she was bid and stepped forward. She inhaled audibly through the nose. Her body shuddered.

"Again," said Viktor, and again she shuddered. Viktor's eyes became abruptly intense—greed made evident in a glint.

"Thank you, Marissa," he said, "that will be all." She exited the room on visibly shaky legs.

"I must have the formula," said Viktor. He slapped a palm against the table. "How much for it?"

The forthrightness caught Julian off his guard. He felt cornered. "It's . . . um . . . still a work in progress," he said evasively.

"Nonsense," said Viktor. "You saw the girl. She all but had an orgasm on her feet.

Hell, for all we know, she did have an orgasm. I'd say the mixture is perfect."

"Well, I'm afraid I'd have to give it some thought," Julian went on, then it occurred to him that if anyone were to get too near the elephant, they would surely discover the source of the scent. He could not let this happen.

"Also," he added quickly, "I'm afraid that I'll need to take Trumpeter back to my workshop for extensive repairs."

"Yes, yes," said Viktor with a dismissive wave of his hand. "Do what you must with the brute, but I say again, I want that formula."

WITH THE HELP of two male stable hands, both of whom wrinkled their noses but refrained from comment, Julian was able to coax Trumpeter into his rolling cage. Though the animal continued to rage once inside, battering the walls and sending forth scalding clouds, the behavior seemed disingenuous now, as if the elephant were an actor growing tired of his part.

Getting Trumpeter back out again and into the workshop proper was another matter. Fortunately, Julian possessed a small grey mouse that made the bull elephant flighty. In the end, it was less a chore than an amusing chase that ended with Trumpeter cornered in his stall and wailing his discontent.

It wasn't until the carriages were out of sight and the mouse had been returned to its countertop that Julian finally allowed himself a sigh of relief. Trumpeter abruptly stopped trumpeting and playfully swished his tail.

"Well, I'll be damned," said Julian. "Aren't you just a clever beast?" Fluid fairly gushed now from the temporal ducts. Julian collected it in cups and pots, later to be transferred to proper ampules. It seemed that old proverb had some substance to it, after all. If destiny so decreed, a loved thing would indeed find its way back again. Moreover, it might even fashion a means by which to stay.

When all was bottled and done, Julian had fifty-eight ampules in his possession.

He immediately drafted a missive to Viktor Krane, stating within that the "malfunction" was actually a fatal flaw in the design, and that while he could, theoretically, bring the elephant around, it would only be temporary. The animal would forever be dangerous, unpredictable. Julian promised a full refund. He also proposed a partnership built around a certain soon-to-be-sought-after perfume. It was a take-it-or-leave-it offer; the formula was not for sale.

Having never been one for boldness, Julian felt exhilarated by adopting such a steadfast position. And really, what could Viktor say in the end but yes?

And so it was that Julian's mechanical family soon began to grow, the elephant and the mouse and the toad joined first by an energetic chipmunk and then by a dancing bear, and then by a project requiring ten long months from design to completion; a companion for a faithful friend; another trumpet in their merry band.

For a period of exactly one week every autumn thereafter, Julian took down the posters and closed down the show while Trumpeter thrashed about wildly within his stall, the episodes of rage insuring that no one would venture close enough to discern the true source of the exotic scent. A scent now recognized far and wide as "Love, Must." ☻

Kurt Kirchmeier lives and writes in Saskatoon, Saskatchewan. His stories have appeared in a variety of magazines and anthologies including *Albedo One, Horror Library Volume 3, Shimmer,* and *Triangulation: Dark Glass.* For more info, visit www.kurtkirchmeier.com.

I·HAVE·TAKEN·INTO·MY CONSIDERATION **MANY THEORIES.**

 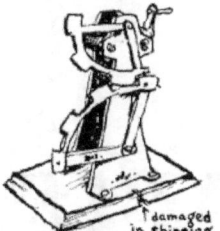

damaged in shipping

G 3638-3639. MODERN, TRADITIONAL

All epicycliod models come with a "GUARANTEED NO SLIPPAGE" certificate. *Celebrate geometry with us.*

"Sleeping, yet ready for the expected foe, I lie concealed within my iron walls; He comes, he feels my iron weapons blow, We fight; I sleep again,—for soon he falls."
—Friedrich Schiller

GOING BACK & FORTH *ALL DAY*

G 3640. Now to slide in a baseboard to prevent doorknob striking the wall.

UNTIL...

G 36"41. Natural forces came upon a lonesome tale.

THEIR·ARRANGEMENT·IS SECONDARY

G 3641   G 36"42

IMPORTANT: ALL LISTED PRODUCTS ARE DORMANT MOTIONS. SEE pg. 9 FOR OUR SELECTION OF ENERGY.

MACHINE PHENOMENA
Watch your Mechanics

EACH SET INCLUDES: A fixed element and one that is free to be moved in a particular way according to the constitution of the pair.

COLLECT ALL **3** FOR VARIETY.
·MOST·KINEMATIC·SET· **SCREW AND NUT**
G 3645.

FROM A TIGHT GRIP...

G3644

TRY TO TURN AWAY...

G3646 IT STILL FALLS OVER YOU.

WHEN **THEY** REACH OUT
G 3643
A parallel link mechanism as seen in the pages of DAVINCI'S mechanical treatise: CODEX MADRID.

THERE IS **NO RETURN**

For the most discreet of motions, think of this famous pair: RACKET G3647 & PAWL

G 3648
WE EXAMINE THE MYSTERY

Inspired by the sciences of cosmic movement, multiple planet gears. A warm ray of torque emits from the central sun gear.

Fit for watch fobs, film projectors, etc. GENEVA MOVEMENT is a thing to behold. INSIDE HERE WE FIND the movement to keep us in step.

BUT FEAR THE INTERMEDIATE SP·ACE......

HARVEY SAYS: "**A STRUCT** IS LONELY: FIND YOUR STRENG..."

FIRE, WATER, WIND SOLD SEPARATELY.

PHORONOMIC HORRORS PLAGUE OUR LIVES *

—bullying deadbolts—
—yawning door hinges—
—condeming sash pulleys—
IS CONVENIENCE WORTH THE RISK? in this case...YES.

HARNESS MISCHIEVIOUS ENERGY. **IRON·WILL HARDWARE**

* motion with no clear origins.

BRILLIANT ~BRAND~ **B** G 3650

A gear that tightens molecules, without shortening the pencil length. As always with **HARVEY'S** products is the strange objects that seem ALL TOO FAMILIAR.

IF THERE IS ANY CAPACITY IN WHICH WE CAN SERVE YOU, THE CONSUMER, DO NOT HESITATE TO WRITE US A NOTE. IT IS IN OUR BEST INTEREST TO KNOW YOU ARE HERE. BROWSING.

HUNGRY GHOSTS

BY JAY LAKE

illustration by Lizard

IN WHICH THE OLD
WORLD'S SPIRITS ARE
RESTLESS, AND THE
NEW WORLD IS NOT
PREPARED FOR THEM

*After trading with the dead, count your horses twice
when the sun next rises.* —APACHE PROVERB

T HE ST. KYRIL mine gaped out of the mountainside cold and
damp as any gate to the next world should be, fogs roiling in
the dark, dank adit that marked the entrance. Peaks towered
in all directions, the high-altitude valley filled with struggling
pines and starving deer and little streams that burbled with
water cold enough to clench a man's gut to muscled knots.

This was a place where bent-backed miners wrestled wealth
from the bowels of mountains, though very little of that wealth
stuck to their fingers. A river of silver ran from here, down into the
lower valleys, and out across the eastward prairies to cities filled
with white men and railroads and guns.

But here, here there was only cold rock and the creaking
shafts beneath the earth. And of late, something that had come
rampaging through the nights against all common sense and at-
tempts to lay it to rest. Word had been sent by unquiet paths—
slit-tongued mountain men and stolid Indians—to Li Cheng-Ho,
who had advised his questioners against certain actions in the
face of ruin. He had been ignored for the Chinese dog that he was,

and so ruin had come to St. Kyril.

Li Cheng-Ho took little satisfaction from the fact that he had been correct.

Now he was cold, and scared, and had been asked to come lay the angry spirits to rest. The brawling, sunny streets of Hisan were a lifetime ago and a world away, with their homey smells of fish and snake, and familiar golden faces on every passer-by. This American land was colder, darker, more terrible than anything he had ever faced in the orange-bricked passages deep beneath the temples of the Celestial Kingdom.

To Chu Jung with the Russians and their schemes.

Now he was faced with a slope of mixed scree and snow, a complex of buildings burned to their floors, and almost a hundred frightened Chinese miners. Peasants, the lot of them, big-muscled, dark-skinned southern illiterates who belonged in the paddies. But still Chinese in their way. Still subjects of the Celestial Emperor even here so far from home. His countrymen stood now with a mix of Russian and Texian overseers, all angry and heavily armed as British sailors in the bargain.

"Ancestors grant I am never this foolish again," he muttered in Cantonese. Then louder, in English, "I go down now, ah? I put hungry ghosts to sleep." His finger stabbed, worn felt blankets flapping over the last rags of his embroidered robes, gold threads long since picked free to sell for food and opium. "You no do this thing again, ah?"

Poliarkov, the mine foreman and a man to whom Li Cheng-Ho had taken an immediate and thorough dislike, growled something in Russian before jerking his thumb at the open shaft. "Get on with you, Chinaman."

"Silver first." Li Cheng-Ho knew what it meant to be Chinese in America.

"On your mother's grave," breathed Poliarkov.

Li Cheng-Ho stood his ground. "If I die, silver still in there. You come fetch it out. If I live, silver for me anyway." He didn't re-

ally need silver for himself. His needs were met by his new friends in the high peaks. But the funds would serve indirectly to repay his debts to those same friends, people who would never understand the concept of money or the value of silver.

Poliarkov pulled a leather bag from beneath the coarse, grubby weave of his billowing Cossack tunic. "Twenty ounces of fine dust," he said with bad grace, then tossed the little sack at Li Cheng-Ho, just far enough to the left that the Chinese mage had to leap for it.

Li Cheng-Ho made a show of opening the bag, checking the quality of the silver dust. He would be cheated on the weight, of course. That went without saying. But he'd demanded twenty ounces expecting twelve or fifteen, and so was not disappointed.

"I do not do this for your filthy money," he said in Cantonese, "but for the sake of the ghosts and my countrymen."

There was a muttering of approval from the assembled miners.

"Speak a real language," growled the foreman.

"A charm. For your safety, ah. Me too."

There was nothing more to say. Li Cheng-Ho stepped to the shadowed opening of the mine, knelt down between the cart rails and laid out his joss sticks.

THE MAGIC OF his youth had been of a metaphorical sort. The old men had proclaimed it in lectures within gold and lacquer halls, the young men had snickered, but they all practiced their arts with a deadly seriousness. No educated man believed in the literal reality of ghosts or demons, any more than they believed in the literal reality of the gods. But those were conversations held in the quiet privacy of walled gardens serviced by whispering eunuchs, not out in the world where anyone might hear.

Including inimical spirits, of course.

So they had sat among the mulberry trees of Hisan, the young men of his genera-

tion—just like the young men of countless generations before—and practiced alectryomancy upon the swallows that wheeled overhead, divined futures for themselves and their families in the swirling of ink and the fall of dust from the wheels of an ox-cart.

It had almost been fun.

Word had come back from the Big Forest, America-across-the-water, that the Russians were hiring laborers by the shipload to build roads and cities and mines in opposition to the British and their wayward American lackeys. The Celestial Kingdom had long been searching for a way to counterbalance British influence in the trading ports of Asia, so accommodations had been reached in silk-paneled rooms deep within the hushed walls of the palaces of the northern and southern capitals.

And so the people left. Every educated man knew that the Celestial Kingdom was home to a river of people so great that should they walk into the sea one by one, there would never be an end to the march. Ships came and went, laborers left their fields or their workshops.

But the tales came home, with the bodies of the few who had found wealth or fortune before they died.

In America, the ghosts were real as rice.

The demons were real.

The gods were real.

So the Lord Abbott, and the Prince-Governor of Hisan, and the nine scholars of the university, had determined they would send young men of good-but-not-too-good family and better education to see what was true in the world and what was merely the rumoring chatter of foreigners. Proficiency with the Eight Legs examination was important, but more important was the inability to buy one's way out of the mission.

Li Cheng-Ho had been too poor to escape.

He had taken a rough, leaky ship to Aleskaya, and spent a year among shouting Russians, learning a little of their language and a little of the English tongue. Speaking

with ignorant barbarians was painful, but none of them could even hear the languages of the Celestial Kingdom.

Then another period in Fort Rossiya above Tomales Bay where the great sharks swam, amid the wheat plantations and the so-called Warm Inuit, the little brown men the Russians had set over their dominions there, to grow the wheat and make war against the Spanish and the English. After that he had traveled east, following the abortive railroads and the caravan trails into the mountains, another human drop in that river of Chinese stepping off the beaches of Shang-Hai and Guang-Jou to spread out across the wild American mountains with its flying men and giant, furred elephants and fearsome monsters from Christian magic amid the deeps of time.

And there he found this truth: wherever the Chinese went in this strange forested land, their gods and ghosts came with them.

LI CHENG-HO stepped past the curtain of incense, into the dark throat of the mine. He had smoked the three sacred herbs, drank of the blood wine, thrown the short lots and the long, and brought himself to see the world of the ghosts. Now he walked with the smallest of lanterns, hooded to cast a narrow circling white glow. White, the color of death.

"I am here," he whispered in Cantonese. Surely these were southern ghosts, not likely to speak the Mandarin of the Imperial court. "I have come to send you to the Celestial Emperor's grace."

One way to think of a ghost was as the world's imperfect memory of someone who had passed on to the lands of the next world. The unforgotten person wanted forgiveness, or a last deed done for them, or simply needed to be told they had passed on.

Another way to think, of course, was of the inauspicious, unlucky vengeance of those who had died early and badly. Much more likely here in America. Especially given the destruction these ghosts had

wrought in the St. Kyril mine.

He was terribly conscious of the rock around him, framed in place by timber, but still a tiny wormhole tunneled into the gut of the mountain by patient men. Cart rails gleamed faintly beneath his feet, and water dripped everywhere. The mine stank of wet rock and the acid tinge of explosives, mixed with traces of rust and blood and the funk of men working too close together for too long.

A faint gray light appeared in the distance. Something moved deeper in the mine. Li Cheng-Ho put one hand on his copper dagger, then let it drop. Weapons were of no use against ghosts. Knowledge was the power here, summoning and banishment, forgiveness of the dead.

Feeding them.

He knelt, and without releasing the lantern, drew forth a moon cake wrapped in lucky red paper. The paper was torn, and worn pink from use, but neither the Russians, the Texians nor the Mormons saw need to make more or trade for it from the Far East, so he was forced to economize.

It was not a disgrace here, Li Cheng-Ho told himself, even though at home poverty was the worst kind of shame.

The moon cake was mealy and damp. Still, he had been able to find sufficient honey to make it properly, and the auspicious characters had been carved into the top of the cake with his copper knife.

"Come eat, and take your rest," he called.

It would not be that easy, Li Cheng-Ho knew. If it were, the ghosts would not have burned the minehead buildings. More was at stake here, some larger grievance on the part of those who had lost their way from the Other World.

The light grew brighter, flickering as it came. Spirits passing before the lamp of another sage? A wind rose, making Li Cheng-Ho glad his lantern was hooded. The air stank of ditchwater and rot, as if a deer had died at the bottom of a well. As little light as there was in here, shadows still danced.

Things came for him. Dead men, or worse.

Li Cheng-Ho stood firm. He had nowhere to run.

"Eat, and tell me what I may do to ease your rest."

The wind gusted hard. A word seemed to come on it, a syllable Li Cheng-Ho did not recognize—pain, complaint, name?— "Bbbbrrrrrrrr."

He wished mightily for his staff, long lost in a flood along some nameless California river. A weapon in its own right, it had also carried great enchantments which would have helped him now.

Then the ghosts were upon him, shuffling shades man-high but less definite in their shape, grave wrappings flapping in the stiff, dank wind, bone-cold fingers brushing at his face, his hands, his clothes.

"I call upon Wang Ti-Tsang and entreat his protection here," Li Cheng-Ho shouted above the moan of the wind. Wang Ti-Tsang was a god of mercy, and one of the few outside the courts of the Other World who could command the dead against their will. "In his name and in the name of the Celestial Emperor I command you to step back and tell me your complaint."

The lantern flared brighter. The ghosts stayed outside the ring of light, so many looming shadow-faced shapes.

Then the word again: "Bbbbrrrrrrr . . ."

So they were not hungry, not as ghosts traditionally were. That word, the wind kept carrying, it was what the English said when they were cold. Li Cheng-Ho had heard that often enough in these benighted mountains. So had the ghosts burned the mine head seeking warmth?

"You have no need to remain in this pit," he told the ghosts. "I release you to the other world."

Bone hands, shattered fingers, wrapped in leathery folds of skin and the rags of old gloves, reached out for him. Though the ghosts still did not step into the lantern's circle, their arms extended inward, so many angular snakes. Li Cheng-Ho was surrounded by a many-limbed monster. It was an inverted spider—all legs and no body.

He made mantic sigils with his free hand, power signs meant for use with demons. "I command you to go!"

The fingers began to pluck at the blankets wrapping his body. It was like being pinched by tiny demons. Each touch burned him, a little spark of pain.

"Away!" bellowed Li Cheng-Ho, finally drawing his useless dagger, but the ghosts still did not heed him. They pressed closer, a wall of rags and bones and icy wind, moaning and wailing their fate, folding him into what they had become, plucking at his wit and his wisdom.

Li Cheng-Ho closed his eyes, thought once more of the Celestial Emperor, and though his body was nigh to dancing with the pain-sparks, once more invoked Wang Ti-Tsang. "Hear me, god of mercy, and spare these ghosts their hunger and their need."

"I hear you," said a voice in perfect court Mandarin, in time with the ringing of tiny bells.

There was a rustle of dead leaves as Li Cheng-Ho opened his eyes. The gray light he had seen before flooded the tunnel. A short man with dark skin and round eyes bent to pick up the abandoned moon cake, accompanied by a cascade of sound. When he looked up again, the newcomer was smiling. He carried a staff covered with metal rings that made the chiming. A glowing pearl at the top shed the gray light.

Li Cheng-Ho bowed. "Master Wang," he said in the same Mandarin.

It was of course the god of mercy in the other world, in his traditional aspect.

"The ghosts do not like this America," Wang Ti-Tsang said around a mouthful of moon cake.

"I am not so taken with it, either."

"I am seeking to lay them to rest, though my efforts are unworthy."

"A greater power than yours or mine disturbs them."

"Master?"

"Burr."

The word again. "Burr?" Li Cheng-Ho asked. He had heard the name. An American Mandarin of some sort.

"He has stolen the secret of endless life. His cheating of death disturbs the ghosts of others. All death is cheated."

Ah, thought Li Cheng-Ho. What he said was: "I am not here to fight in the English wars."

"Burr must be laid to rest." Wang Ti-Tsang handed his staff to Li Cheng-Ho. "I walk in shadows. You walk beneath the sun. Take my power and travel into the dawn until you meet the flower of the east."

"What . . . " Li Cheng-Ho began to ask, but like that he was alone with the dripping water and groaning rock of the St. Kyril mine. The ghosts were gone as if they had never been.

Except for the staff in his hand. The rings jingled silver, and the pearl alone would be worth the ransom of a city. He tried to find a way to extinguish the gray glow, and finally settled for tearing a strip from one of his blankets and wrapping it up.

Li Cheng-Ho did not particularly look forward to explaining himself to Poliarkov, though in truth the ghosts were gone. He checked the pouch of silver dust at his belt. Before he headed east in obedience to the god's word, he had his friends in the high places to repay for their kindnesses.

He missed the Celestial Kingdom most sorely in that moment, where ghosts and gods were safely transitory. ℰ

Jay Lake lives in Portland, Oregon. His recent novels are *Pinion* (concluding the *Mainspring* clockpunk trilogy from Tor Books), *Green* (Tor), *Madness of Flowers* (Night Shade), and *Death of a Starship* (MonkeyBrain). His short fiction appears regularly in literary and genre markets worldwide. Jay is a winner of the John W. Campbell Award and a multiple nominee for the Hugo and World Fantasy Awards.

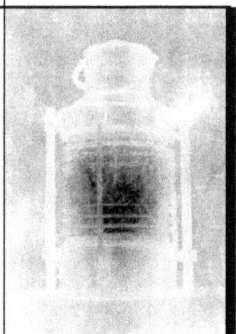

GINGERBREAD HOUSE

BY KATER CHEEK

illustration by Asya Yordanova

IN WHICH A GROUP
OF HOUSEMATES
STOP BEING POLITE
AND START GETTING
REAL HUNGRY

AUGUST 27TH: This house stinks of cinnamon and nutmeg and clove and ginger. The smell clings to everything, even to this journal. My hands are always sticky, and the walls are humming with bees both inside and out. We had a rainstorm last week and the water dripped down the windows, melting holes in the sugar-glass. I hate this house.

It's been three weeks since the missed shipment. Josh thinks they got delayed by a storm or something. Brian says that it's probably a funding issue, like maybe the production company got bought by another company, and the show is up in the air right now. Craig doesn't say anything, but he tore down one of the cameras to try to make a radio. He can probably do it, he's geeky like that, but it's a waste of time. Even if he can get it to work, it won't mean anything. If they wanted to get us, they know where we are.

Brian's been talking about walking to civilization, but I was like, what civilization? We don't even know where we are, and anyway, it's easy to get lost in the woods. Brian goes out anyway, to scout around he says, but he always comes back before dark. When it's dark here, it's *really* dark, and you can't see your hand in front of your face. I haven't gone farther than the outhouse. I'm not the outdoorsy type.

I reread my journals from before the missing shipment. All those stupid competitions, the bake-offs, the architecture contests. I was so proud of myself that I'd outlasted all the others on account of my professional baking skills, so smug that young women don't learn their way around a kitchen anymore. Makes me want to take the earlier me and shake her, make her trade places with that lucky bitch Theresa who sprained her ankle and got a free ride home. Theresa cried when she left, because she wanted that prize money so badly. She can have it. I just want to get out of here.

I ran out of tampons this week. It's bad enough we have an outhouse and have to bathe at the stream, but now I have a colossal nuisance that's mine alone. We all stink, and the house smells like a combination of gym socks and snickerdoodles.

SEPTEMBER 1ST: Spent most of this week baking loaves to wall off Josh's bay window. He got mad at me; he's so proud of it. I like Josh, and the window is pretty, but the sugar-glass is all melting in the humidity, and I'm tired of bees flying in. Josh and Brian were talking about allergies, and what they'd do if they got stung. Brian said he was allergic, and Josh wanted to know how you'd find out you were allergic if you'd never been stung. Craig, as usual, said nothing. He's still fiddling with his radio.

Josh wants to knock down some of the internal walls and open this place up. I agree that we hardly need seven bedrooms (well, six bedrooms and one room for storage) for the four of us. Josh kept going on about feng shui and open space. I think he still talks to the cameras, like he's going to win points for his architectural savvy. Brian said we need to make this house stronger, not tear it down, and since Josh does what Brian wants, he agreed.

Usually Brian just paces around, complaining and smashing things when he gets frustrated. That and make forays into the woods. Now that we don't need him to heft heavy cake-panels anymore, he's decided to be Mr. Outdoorsman. Whatever. As long as he stops bothering me.

SEPTEMBER 4TH: Josh finally stopped using his bedroom and let me wall it up. Before the last shipment he'd been fixing it up with Florentine swirls of icing in pale pinks and blues, peppermint candy wainscoting, and mullions for the window formed out of red licorice. They'd photographed the hell out of it the last time the producers were here, said that was just the thing to boost ratings. Josh got to stay on past the third round on account of his bedroom. He's still proud of it, even though that room is part of what kept him on. It's like the thing with the bay window. He doesn't care about the bugs flying in, he just wants to keep his art from getting destroyed. I told him he cared more about his art than his life, and he said he did. Freak.

I stopped staying in my bedroom too. The nights are warm, and the smell of candy and spice gets overwhelmingly cloying when the door is shut. There was a gnawing sound, and when we pulled off some of the peppermint wainscoting we found nests of mice digging burrows for themselves in the outside wall. The house is alive. Crawling with mice by night, buzzing with bees by day. If it weren't for the solid timber roof we'd be sleeping rough, because the mice and bees seem to eat the walls as fast as I can bake them. I tried whitewashing the outside with icing glue, but there isn't enough meringue powder. There are dead bees stuck to the walls, embedded from when the sugar half melted.

We've been living off the last of the stew packets and pancakes since you can't make much else with egg powder and flour. The pancakes are kind of mealy and flavorless, since the flour is the cheapest crappi-

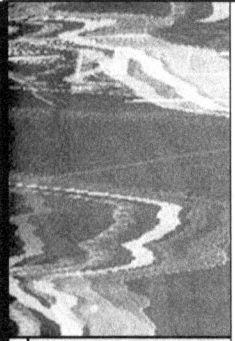

est stuff you can imagine. They warned us not to eat it, said it had some 'not for human consumption' preservatives in it, but what are we going to do? The pancakes tasted like papier mâché the first time, and they don't taste any better the tenth day running, but we don't have much else. Josh and Brian and Craig eat candy sometimes, but I never want to see candy again.

SEPTEMBER 12TH: The stew packets are all gone. Brian found some berries today. Josh didn't want to eat them because he said we didn't know what they were, but we ate them anyway. They were so sour they made our mouths pucker, but we're sick of pancakes, and it's not like we don't have plenty of sugar to go with it. Brian made a bow and said he's going hunting later. I haven't seen anything larger than a rabbit since we got here, but the thought of meat makes my mouth fill with spit. I've been taking my vitamins, but I still feel anemic.

Craig can't get a signal on his radio, probably because we're too far away from any city. Josh thinks we're in Canada, but if we were in Canada, we'd at least see planes fly overhead, wouldn't we? None of us really know exactly where we are. So even if we had a car and drove all day, we'd still be in Podunk nowhere.

I miss civilization. I even miss the smog. Here it's always peppermint and gingerbread and fir and pine, which I'll now associate with loneliness and hunger forever. This stupid show has ruined Christmas for me.

Brian goes on and on about how he's going to sue their asses off, and how he bets that his dad has already hired a lawyer to make the producers rescue us. I told him he's smoking crack. It's obvious that something really bad happened, not just to the show but to everyone. Josh overheard me saying that and he got really upset, left in a huff. Brian told me to shut the fuck up, and

it looked like he was going to hit me, but he left. I thought I saw Craig roll his eyes.

Since then, Brian spends most of his days out wandering in the forest. I'm glad. When he's around here, he just fights with everyone. Josh and Brian seem to have an alliance against me, even though we aren't really competing any more. For me the game was over the first time they missed a shipment. I overheard Josh talking to the camera, reciting a poem for his girlfriend. I didn't say anything, but Brian got on me for eavesdropping. Where am I supposed to go? We're in a 24' x 24' cake box with half of it walled off!

I spend most of my days baking, trying to shore up the sagging walls. I tried using some of the soggy baked bricks as filler, reworking the crumbs into the loaves. Josh said it was disgusting, but it's not like we're going to eat the damn things. At least the storage room is still full: Seventeen kilos of egg powder, four hundred kilos of flour, eighty kilos of sugar, almost three kilos of baking soda. Twelve cans of artificial spice blend. Plenty of candy. Salt's just about gone. More than enough to last us until the end of the month, but what if they don't come by then? Today I started breaking my vitamins in half so they'll last longer.

Craig just started broadcasting S-O-S. The thing crackles like thunder every time he taps it, and it's going to get real old, real fast. I haven't said anything about it. We all have to do things to keep us occupied, keep us from remembering that we're stuck in a gingerbread prison in the wilderness, as helpless as pets in a locked car.

Josh took one of the paring knives and started chip carving the wooden furniture. He's quite talented at this, too, and the medieval-looking flourishes make up for the fact that we can't go in his tower anymore. He said he was thinking a—

Brian just came home, and he has a leg of venison!

* * *

SEPTEMBER 16TH: Just reread the last journal entry, and started getting hungry again at the memory of the deer meat, even though it made us all sick. Brian said he shot the deer, but when I went out there later it was pretty obvious that he just found carrion. It must have been sitting there for a few days, because ravens and some kind of predator had carried off most of it. Honestly, I'd still eat more, if there were any left. I'm sick to death of pancakes and berries.

SEPTEMBER 19TH: Brian said all the berry bushes are gone. He claims that the bears ate them, however no one saw a bear but him. Maybe he just ate all the berries for himself. I could try to find some myself, but someone has to stay here and keep baking. Seems like every day there's a new hole in the wall that has to be repaired.

Josh isn't doing well. He cries a lot, shaking himself back and forth. Brian practically growls at me if I get near him. Those two make Craig seem normal. Craig has a paperback novel he brought, and he reads it all the time. I asked if I could read it when he was done, and he just shook his head. I decided not to push the issue. I have enough enemies in this house as it is.

SEPTEMBER 21ST: We had a storm last night, and the entire north wall collapsed on itself. The trees were closer on that side, and I think that the branches were sluicing rainwater against the wall. A rivulet of water undercut the foundation, and Brian says that's what made the wall collapse, but he's full of shit. It was just crappy building, that's all.

It was obvious, even to Brian, that we had to rebuild the wall and fast. Summer's over, and the oven is the only source of heat. The producers didn't give us any shovels or hoes, so we used baking sheets and loaf pans. One of the loaf pans got ruined, which meant I could only bake three at a time. Josh helped mortar them in, until I caught him making pastel curlicues and yelled at him. This crap is the only thing we have to build with, unless they can figure out how to make a log cabin with nothing but pocket knives, and Josh hasn't gotten it through his head that no one cares about his artistic side anymore. Then Brian and even Craig got on my case, but they don't understand how important it is not to waste. We had a big blowup. Finally I got fed up and went for a walk. I got a little turned around, and Brian took it upon himself to come and find me. Now he's acting like he saved me, which makes him even more insufferable. Maybe Craig has the right idea. I should just not say anything.

SEPTEMBER 23RD: The bees are gone, but there are more mice than ever. Craig made a mousetrap, and even though we bait it with candy, he gets about a mouse a day. Brian and I sharpened metal spatulas and take turns killing the ones we see. They're fast little buggers, but there are so many of them that we kill at least three a day by luck alone. They gnaw through the walls at night, and sometimes they die and rot. Rotting mice, feces, gingerbread, and human stench. Sometimes we have to open a door just so we don't suffocate on the reek.

Craig started making beer, which means that, at some level, he has accepted that we're trapped here. Josh still thinks they're watching us through the cameras, that they're doing all of this for ratings. Brian wants us to pack up and go, says that every day we stay here we play right into their hands. I told him he's full of it. He was up all night talking to Craig about it, but Craig's not stupid. Wander off in to the woods in autumn? Might as well slit our wrists now.

I told them that we have to be patient, that they can't leave us here forever, but what are we going to do if they don't get us before winter? The generator still works, enough to power the lights, and the gas line is strangely reliable, so we can keep the oven on to heat the house, but we have to keep the door open or we'll suffocate.

On the plus side, mice are tasty. We had mice soup with our pancakes tonight. Josh wouldn't eat any, but he'll change his mind eventually. I hate the bones, but it's nice to have meat.

SEPTEMBER 26TH: Craig over boiled the yeast, or it was the wrong kind of yeast, or something. So, no beer.

The nights have been getting chillier. Josh wanted to run the oven all night, but I said we might suffocate from the gas. Craig backed me up. We pushed all the beds together, to conserve warmth. Brian still thinks we should all go, before winter hits. I thought he was done talking about it, but apparently not. He's crazy. Where would we go, anyway? Brian says he thought he saw smoke to the south, but I haven't seen anything. Josh doesn't sound like he wants to go, and I don't think Brian will go alone. Don't know about Craig. Craig never says anything. He started taking apart another camera, fiddling with it. God knows what good he thinks its going to do.

SEPTEMBER 30TH: Josh and Brian left. They must have planned it in secret, because we didn't even hear them pack. Craig pointed out their tracks in the dust of the yard. I ran out to look for them, try to talk some sense into them, but you don't have to go very far in the forest before it all starts to look the same.

They took half the sheets and blankets, a kilo of flour each, and most of our egg powder. I thought they took the salt too, but I found it this afternoon. Brian can go

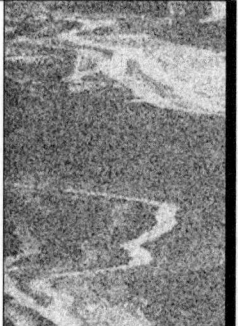

fuck himself, but when I think of Josh, piping rosettes onto a shutter, or the way he'd peer out at you from behind his bangs, it makes me want to cry. I hope they come back, but it's been a day and a half.

Cold snap must have come through, because all of a sudden the temperatures are below freezing all day. The walls have swelled up in places from the ice, and the sugar-glass windows shattered, but except for that the house seems to be holding up. Craig and I took the extra mattresses and leaned them up against the walls.

OCTOBER 2ND: As far as I'm concerned, it's winter already. The pipes are only unfrozen for a couple hours a day, so I fill up every container we have with water, and store it as cubes just outside.

Was thinking about Brian and Josh today. Maybe if Brian and I hadn't fought, they'd still be here. Got really depressed and started crying, but I was outside so Craig didn't see. The tears froze on my cheeks. I try not to go outside very often, because of the chilblains. Craig has a rash on his skin, little red dots at the base of his hairs, and he thinks its frostbite. I don't know what frostbite looks like, but we'll find out soon enough.

I'm tired all the time. Even Craig's been shuffling around like an old man, and he's not even thirty.

OCTOBER 5TH: Craig and I decided to leave the oven running all night. Woke up and hadn't suffocated, so that's going to be the plan from now on. Half the pans are rusted and bent from being used to clear away the ruined wall, and we don't have water unless we use the crème brûlée torch to heat the pipes, but the oven still works fine. Thank God for the oven.

OCTOBER 7TH: Craig went into a rage and destroyed all the cameras. Scared the shit out of me. I kept thinking of him as

this quiet little geek, and his anger came out of nowhere. He was thrashing around, ripping up everything he saw. I got so scared I left, but outside it's so cold that I felt like I was inhaling shards of glass, so I came back inside after an hour or so. Craig looked embarrassed, but of course he didn't say anything. I didn't say anything either. I'm still shaking. I don't want to set him off again. Cameras are all busted for good, so even if Josh was right and they were still watching, they aren't anymore.

It's colder than I ever thought possible. We're wearing every piece of clothing we brought, and half the sheets too. One of the light bulbs burned out, so we moved into the kitchen, and put the extra mattresses against the wall to the common room. Now that the bulb is burned out, we can only see in the kitchen. I killed a couple of mice in there, but they're getting wary. Maybe they're hibernating or something. I wish I could hibernate.

We took the largest mixing bowl and started using it as a chamber pot so we wouldn't have to go outside. It's still cold in the common room, so cold that ice forms on the top of the bowl, and your pee melts a hole in it. You have to be careful not to touch anything metal with your skin. I accidentally touched one of the baking sheets and Craig had to pour hot water on it to get it off me.

Craig's been nicer since he blew up. I think he feels guilty.

OCTOBER 11TH: Craig is sick. He threw up a couple times, and he doesn't seem to know where he is, though he hasn't got a fever or anything. I wonder if he's been sick for a while and I just now noticed. He tried to get out of bed, to do what I don't know, but he fell over and couldn't climb up again. I've been heating up water for him to drink, and making sure he still eats, though there's nothing but pancakes, candy, and gingerbread bricks.

I don't know if it's catching or not.

My period's a week late. Two, actually, come to think of it. Haven't had sex, so it's probably stress.

OCTOBER 16TH: Woke up last night unable to breathe. The mattress had fallen over the door to the common room, sealing us in. The mattress doesn't stay up well, and there's nothing to keep this from happening again, but we can't turn the oven off or we'll freeze to death. Sometimes I think we'll freeze to death anyway. If the gas runs out, we'll be dead in hours.

Craig hasn't gotten out of bed. He doesn't seem to know where he is or who I am, and he says he's hungry but he won't eat anything. No fever, so maybe it's not a virus? I don't really know what's going on.

We're out of egg powder, so now the only thing to eat is flour and water. Even with good flour it would taste like crap, but this stuff is probably cut with chalk or something. It tastes like library paste.

OCTOBER 20TH: Craig's been getting worse and worse. He's got a sniffle now too, and seems to have trouble breathing, and while I was helping him go to the bathroom I saw he had that reddish rash all over his body. Even his gums are bleeding. It's scary and horrible and the worst part is that I feel sorry for myself. Here he is, sick and maybe dying in some godforsaken forest out in the middle of nowhere, and all I can think of is how terrified I am that he'll die and leave me here.

OCTOBER 28TH: Craig died. It took hours. He gasped and gasped until finally he stopped, and there were nothing I could do about it except hold his hand and wipe his forehead. I dragged his body outside, but I couldn't get it very far because he's heavy and it's so cold I feel like I'm freezing solid. There isn't even any winter gear, just fifteen tee shirts wrapped around my arms

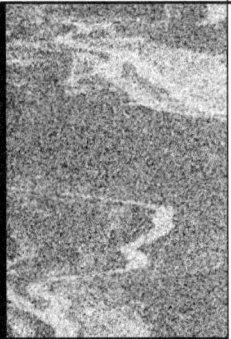

and three pair of jeans which make me walk like a robot. I dragged him maybe twenty feet, and tried to make a cairn or something but my hands wouldn't work well in this cold so I had to go back inside every ten minutes. I put my hands inside the oven and when the feeling came back to my fingers I started screaming in agony. I don't want to go outside again.

I tried eating gingerbread, but it's so hard to chew it makes my teeth feel like they're going to fall out.

This pen is almost out of ink. I ransacked Craig's belongings, and found a paperback novel, but no pen. No vitamins either, not even an empty jar. He must not have brought any. I read the novel twice already. It sucks, but I'll proably read it a third time.

Craig's driver's license said he was only twenty four. Jesus, he was just a kid.

DON'T KNOW WHAT date it is. Lost track.

I've read Craig's paperback six times now. It's one of the worst novels I've ever read, and now I've memorized whole passages from it. That's pretty much my life right now. Sleep, read, sleep, eat. I can't even bake anymore, not that there's much left to bake, because the oven can't get hot enough. I leave it running all the time with the door open. It's like a race between the oven's ability to heat the house and the walls' ability to steal the heat away.

Not as much snow as I thought there'd be. It drifts up against the walls, but it's more like beach sand than the wet flakes they have in Buffalo. Most of the wind comes from the side of the house near Josh's bedroom, so I put an airhole in the opposite side, right next to his bay window. It's too cold with the door left open. If Josh were here, he'd probably make a stained glass casement window out of sugar. There are still a few bottles of food coloring. Maybe I could do something like that. It's

better than wasting more time on that crappy novel.

THE WINDOW IDEA didn't work. The sugar sticks to the pans if you don't use parchment paper, and we ran out of that a long time ago. My fingers are sore from trying to work in the cold, and the last baking sheet is pretty much ruined. I miss Josh. I even miss Brian.

I try not to think about Craig.

I dreamt last night that Brian came back with a giant leg of venison. I dream about food, about oranges and hamburgers and strawberries and hot wings from my favorite bar. Beer too. I'd kill for some beer. I'd kill for some meat. I'm so sick of pancakes. Every time I make another one I have to force myself to eat it, then concentrate to keep from puking it up again. I even miss the mice.

It's so fucking cold that today I took the racks out of the oven and climbed inside. I've lost so much weight that I'm just barely able to fit. I probably would have slept in there, but my hair got singed from getting too close to the flames.

I DECIDED I couldn't stand it anymore. I put on all the clothes I could find, packed up a sack of food, and headed out into the woods. The forest was perfectly still, and not easy to travel, because there are bushes everywhere and you have to fight your way through them. I left a couple hours before dawn, using the stars to help me find south, and I kept walking past mid day.

I'd been walking for several hours before I smelled the smoke. You can't see much in the forest cause the trees are so thick, and I think that's what saved me. That, and shyness. I haven't spoken since Craig died, and it wasn't like he and I talked that much. I sat there for what must have been a half hour, just watching them.

They have a tiny little trailer, white with aluminum siding and patches of plywood over the windows. The roof is corrugated tin. It must not keep the heat in well, because water was dripping down icicles on the edge of the roof. There were at least four kids, mean eyed things wearing nothing more than rags. Here I was, freezing to death wearing every piece of clothing I owned, and these kids were gathering twigs wearing what looked like jeans and overcoats. They had fur hats on, but except for one kid who had a blue scarf, they wore nothing over their faces, and everyone's mouth had frozen into a half sneer of mucus. The woman had a baby on her hip, swaddled in rags, and she screeched orders at the children, swatting them when they moved too slowly. There was a man there too, carrying a hatchet. He yelled at her, and she yelled back, screaming louder and louder until he raised the hatchet, at which point she got quiet.

They didn't look friendly at all, but I was so lonely I thought about calling out to them. I sat hunched, shivering behind the fir tree, trying to make up my mind, until I saw something that made me feel even colder.

Brian's glasses, glinting in the puddle that formed under the roof.

And suddenly it occurred to me that Josh had owned a blue scarf.

I turned and slipped away as silently as my terrified body would let me. I ran as much as I could. I don't think they saw me. I hoped they didn't see me. Please God let them not have seen me.

I thought I might have gotten lost on the way back, but I'd made a large enough path in the snow that I was able to follow it even in the moonlight. It took me hours. Maybe it was far enough away. Maybe it would snow and cover my tracks.

Inside the house it smelled sweet and warm. I put my hands and feet in the oven to get feeling back in them, tolerating the agony of recirculation in silence. Who knows how far sound carries in the woods?

Right now I'm sucking on candy and shivering next to the oven door. Here in the house it feels safer. It will snow overnight. My tracks will be covered. They won't follow me.

IT DIDN'T SNOW. The children are here, two of them, lean like feral wolves. They're eating on the house right now, but sooner or later they'll make their way inside. I've disassembled one of Craig's radios and I fastened one end of the wire to the bed. It's strong enough to hold a child, I think. I can imprison them for a while, buy some time until I think of what to do. It's a shitty plan, but it's better than no plan at all. ☺

Kater Cheek is a graduate of Clarion San Diego, class of 2007. Her short fiction can be found in various journals and anthologies. She has a B.A. in linguistics, a brown belt in karate, and a desert garden that doesn't yield nearly as much as she would like. When not writing, she throws pots, paints, binds books, and plays with molten glass. She keeps an artblog at www.catherinecheek.com and a webcomic about chickens at www.coopdegrace.com.

DEDALUS AND THE LABYRINTH

BY J.M. McDERMOTT

illustration by Ming Doyle

IN WHICH WE ARE ALWAYS THREATENED BY DEATH FROM ABOVE, BUT WE NONETHELESS SHALL GAZE SKYWARD

DON'T GET LOST *in the labyrinth.* That's what your father always told you. Stick to the human's fractured groves among the warped vines and stones. Pick berries with your mother in the known halls. Hunt for birds with your father's nets. Stick together and never let yourself get separated from your group. The goblins are the most terrifying things here in their clouds of mystery and darkness, but they are only one of a million ways to die in these stone halls and pagan tessaracts.

Do not wander past the watchmen into the sandstone walls where the minotaurs send out their little hunting parties and place traps. Do not dip your toes into the winding pools of the marshy limestones where the mermaids latch their teeth into your skin like leeches and pull you down into the deep waters to your death.

And the goblin city? Who knows what dangers will devour your flesh if you are foolish enough to crawl around looking for the goblin city. You'll never reach the city. If you do, it will certainly be the worst fate of all. Death is what awaits all who explore the curving halls and pagan tessaracts within tessaracts within tessaracts of warped space and time and unending halls of stone.

We have made our place here, in our stretch of halls, and we must hold it as best we can.

You asked your father—I heard it though you did not know I was listening—if there was ever a place in the labyrinth that had no walls, no stones, no bending and twisting paths carved into the rocky hills. He told you that the only open field was in the goblin city. He assured you that searching out the goblin city was the road to death.

Your father should have taken his own advice. He went hunting for the goblin city when your sister was taken—like your girls are occasionally taken. He fashioned a brickbat from a fallen stone and charged through the sandstone halls wearing his death all over his face. I saw the minotaurs snare him.

Do not be mistaken by their beastly heads. Minotaurs are actually very intelligent animals. They know the herding ways of men with hands. While your father swung his brickbat, two lassoes from two angles caught his feet and hands. They dragged him to their fires. They roasted your father and ate him—and I'm very sorry to tell you that.

Your uncle led your little tribe of a dozen families. He burned ropes in mourning for the lost man and the lost girls—your sister and your father. The women wailed.

In the morning, the village had to continue.

Your uncle had the women re-fashion bird nets to use as traps when the goblins came for the girls again next year. These nets, of course, would not work. Every generation tries it once or twice. Still, it was smarter than what your father had done.

Sometimes men, like your father, had gone searching for the girls that were taken by the goblins.

Those poor stolen girls would birth more goblins and labyrinth beasts after the Samhain orgies impregnated them all. Little girls were best, always virginal. They came from everywhere little girls come from. They come from the world of men, and from the men of the labyrinth, and from any other place girls happen to be—like where I had come from. And, the girls never went home after they were filled up with that goblin absence.

I'm sorry about your sister, too, but there was nothing I could do about it. It happens every year. Your tribe went to sleep some night near Samhain, and when you woke up a girl or two or three were gone. You can place all the vigils you want. You can hide the girls. You can arm them to the teeth. It doesn't matter. The goblins come in the dark. All the lights snuff out. Men swing brickbats and rusty old swords at voids and can do nothing to stop the creatures that exist in that awful absence.

When the starlight and moonlight and sunlight return, a girl or two or three are gone. Mothers fall into the arms of fathers and weep to the fates in rivers. Young boys reach out their hands to their one, true love, and she isn't there anymore, and her fate is as awful as any in this awful place.

The labyrinth is dangerous. Your ancestors knew this. They came here in groups and bunches, and armies, searching for their own lost sisters and daughters. The ones that survived the experience were the ones that gave up and found each other and fought for a place among fruit-bearing trees and vines where birds fly overhead all seasons.

I remember the day after your father died searching for your sister—when your mother was all that was left to you—when you first climbed a stone wall to peer over the top and see what you could see of your world. A maze of stone and vine halls rolled off into the curve of the horizon as far as you could see. There was no sign of the goblin city from here. Slight movements in the rocks indicated the presence of beasts and creatures. Inside the sandstone walls, you saw the high, sharp tips of bull horns. Undoubtedly you watched Minotaurs that had so recently taken your father for their supper. In the limestone and granite, other subtle movements at the tip of the rocks indicated signs of life.

You studied them until your mother saw you with your head above the rocks. She screamed and snatched you down hard.

Harpies, she said, *and maybe worse. Who knew what foul creatures flew through the air, searching for children to carry away? Who knew what foul creatures peered over the rocks to find their supper?* She had heard a story from her grandmother about a giant snake that no one could kill that had slipped over the walls in the night and swallowed three men whole before anyone knew what had happened. Just as quickly as it had appeared, the snake melted over the walls again.

At this, brave little soul, you decided it was time to get higher in the air, to see further through the twisting stones and trees. You wanted to see the goblin city. Was it because you wanted to save your sister or because you were merely curious? I do not know. I know only the result, and I choose not to thoroughly question your motivations.

Perhaps the quest was all things to you. Perhaps you were both deathly curious to gaze past the mossy stones and grapevines and bird nets and past the watchmen that hold the evils of the labyrinth back from the narrow corners in the halls.

You wanted to see beyond where two men with spears could drive off terrible minotaurs. You wanted to gaze above the other place where a fire of dried dung fills a long enclosed corridor and no one tells anyone exactly why that corridor must be kept full of the stink at all costs. The watchmen that shout for help and whose voices echo through the stone halls sometimes get killed, like your father. Sometimes a minotaur is just fast enough, just sly enough, to snag a watchman with a lasso and drag him away from his fellows, or a mermaid slips a trap over a wall where a patrolman walks searching for traps to

cut away—and fails, and dies. You've heard those screams in the night. You've been woken to the sound of news traveling back of a man lost. Everyone has.

And you are so sick of the slow death of your friends and family, and so deadly curious to see all things and gaze into the hidden places in the halls and to rise above all that death.

You do not tell others what you are doing.

When the birds come down from the nets along the vines and windy hallways, you snuck away the feathers from the pluckings. You told your mother you were going to make a soft mattress when she found your collection, but she knew that you had the wrong kind of feathers for that. Mattresses were made of down feathers. Fletching was made from the kind of feathers you collected.

She let you keep them, though, hidden in your corner in a large canvas sack that you used like a pillow. You checked it each day for the ants that might come looking for the smell of death.

You left the playing trees where the children spent their days. You went to the nets, like a man should. You gathered birds down from the nets carefully, trying to study their wings and learn what you could of their mystical flight.

For creatures trapped in stone your tribe of survivors, I can only imagine what the birds must seem like. Birds could skip from wall to wall as casually as turning around. They soared over the hills and valleys of dangerous stone. Undoubtedly, they escape the deadly traps and monsters of the halls. All the secrets that slipped their pulsing traps between the stones like invisible throats are no threat to the birds. Only those birds that fly into the nets die. The birds, unused to danger in the sky, fall victim to humble nets and wriggle angrily that anything would stop their wings. How dare the sky refuse them? How dare

anything come to hold them in a labyrinth of tiny vines?

(You and your earth-bound mortals plucked them from the freedom of flight, tore their feathers from their body, roasted them and burned the shit you made when you ate them down a long, dark hall of nightmares.)

You collected the wingbones, too. You spread them out in a moonlit corner in the dark. You listened to the sounds of your little tribe sleeping in the night.

(I watched over your shoulder, but you did not see me.)

You slipped into the shadows alone—a clear violation of your father's advice—to twist the vines and nets and all of your feathers together. You used dried mucus from your own snotty nose and bits of damp moss and vine knots to hold the joints and feathers down.

The wings you made in the darkness there didn't work. I knew they wouldn't. They were far too short, and the elbows did not flex correctly. You had not calculated the weights of birds like you should have, child. You only estimated the size of the body with the size of the wings. You made yourself look like a bird, foolish child, but this wasn't enough.

I suspect your mother did not bother you with this foolishness because like all mothers she assumed that her child—once frustrated—would wander off to other things like children do.

She had berries to gather and other men of your little tribe vying for her. This humble pursuit of yours doomed to failure was fine to keep you busy until you were done mourning your father and your sister.

You built larger wings of twisting ropes and stolen feathers.

Your mother was already pregnant with another daughter. Did she tell you or did she merely wander off into the arms of another man's family? Her belly pushed against her dress. She held a man's hand,

and wandered after him instead of you. You let her wander off. You found a new place to sleep among the young women and young men. You were just a relic to her—I imagine—of a lost daughter and a lost lover, and you were old enough to fend for yourself in this maze where the young must grow up fast.

Her grief was strong enough to give up on you, child.

I DID NOT GIVE up on you, lost child. I watched over you though no one else did. I turned the eyes of harpies away from you. I bent the lassoes of the minotaurs that they had tossed over the walls for lone stragglers like you in these bending halls. I pushed back the awful, unknowable darkness that slithered through the long halls where your shit no longer burned. I stayed the mermaid's hands when your ankles approached the edges of the waters.

I waited for you, child.

You built larger wings with vine ropes to manage the joints. You built even larger wings with a long tail to straighten your path. Finally, you built wings so large a mere breeze would tumble you head over head, and the vine ropes in your hands extended like a puppeteer's strings to the distant tip. You stood on the top of the stone walls with a rope between your teeth to hold you down. Your kite's tail dragged behind you and your motley vine and feather wings looked to all the maze like all the birds of the labyrinth in all their colors had birthed a single monster.

I blew the wind that picked you up.

You caught my gust breath from my hidden tower. You flapped your wings hard and took to the sky. The vines bent and crackled. Feathers that were not lashed down tight enough dripped away like falling leaves.

You flew up higher. You pulled hard on the vines. You spun around in the strong winds and gazed all around you at the hills and valleys of twisting stones. You saw the great beasts of the stones—not just the minotaurs. You saw the giant snake that slid over the walls chasing after the terrified trolls among the cliff paths. You saw the fairy forest, with the tree villages that branched over the walls among the high tree branches. You saw the great kraken's shadow hidden in the deepest trenches of the mermaid's marshland. There, you also saw the mountain of the damned. There, the bone king waited for his resurrection with his army of stalwart skeletons. Over there, the dwarves refashioned the labyrinth's stone walls into forts and castles and they pointed their trebuchets at anything that moved too close to their balustrades.

Higher, you climbed, with the wind that carried you until the horizon spread for centuries and you saw the beginning of the labyrinth and the end of the labyrinth and the center of the labyrinth of the dread goblin city, full of the teeming nightmare hordes alive in their absence of light. You saw the sun. You saw the moon. You saw them merge into a single eclipse in the clouds. You saw the angles where tessaracts and stone melted together into one mystery of time.

I carried you up into my tower in my high parallax turrets.

I am Dedalus, the goblin king.

I flew here ages ago from the land of the dead, searching for my stolen daughter, Icarus. She was taken in the night sleep when the goblins came for our virgin daughters. I chased them. I fell in among the bone king's undead hordes. I fashioned wings, like you did—but mine were made of clouds and smoke.

I landed upon the highest turret in the king's castle, and I dueled the ultimate absence of light with lightning that I had torn from the goblin king's own clouds. I gathered his shattered bones to fashion my own new wings of awful glory.

Goblins bow to me now. They bring me the daughters they steal as offerings to the greatest monster they have ever known. I

horde the girls in my palace, until I can find a way to send them home. I keep the species separated from each other with the very tessaracts of death itself. Whole colonies of lonely girls are locked away here and I have no way of either destroying all the goblins in their terrible city, or transporting all these girls home from my throne.

I have been waiting for you, child.

I watched you fly up and up into the sunlight. I watched the feathers in your wake, falling like leaves as the jet streams devoured your wings. I watched the death fear fill your face.

I reached out a hand through the winds and plucked you from the sky like I could not have done for my own daughter when she flew high like you did—like when the goblins plucked her from her eternal slumber.

I will watch through the goblin king's dismembered eyes for more children like you, who long for freedom in the sky and wander off alone and build their wings.

Someday there will be enough children like you, thousands of them. Then we shall strike down the very monsters that built this place with their hands of absence. We will strike at them with lightning swords until their bodies lay scattered in pieces across the ruined stones.

And we will soar over the labyrinth.

We will solve this maze with battering rams. We will demolish this world of death and misery and secrets.

We will open every portal.

We will breech every wall.

We will fly away home. ☙

J.M. McDermott's first novel *Last Dragon* was no. 6 on Amazon.com's Year's Best Science Fiction and Fantasy of 2008, was shortlisted for a Crawford Prize, and made *Locus*'s Recommended Reading List. His short fiction is appearing or forthcoming in *Fantasy Magazine*, *Lady Churchill's Rosebud Wristlet*, and *Brain Harvest*, among numerous other places.

AS RECORDED ON BRASS CYLINDERS: ADAGIO FOR TWO DANCERS

BY JAMES L. GRANT & LISA MANTCHEV

illustration by Paul Sizer

IN WHICH FINELY CRAFTED LIMBS AND GEARS CANNOT OBSCURE THE BEAT OF A TRUE HEART

I**T WAS THE** kind of American city that hadn't been around for very long, not in the manner it presented itself. The town had existed when Colorado had become an official State, true, but for hundreds of years it had been little more than a place for ruffians and ne'er-do-wells to trade furs, gold, and goods.

For a very short period, Denver had thrived on great inventions. Angelus remembered the first time he'd been sent here, to speak with a brilliant man named Nikolai. The Fifth Empire had been young. Its request had offered the young madman gold, riches, power; Angelus had made the presentation in person. But the brilliant Serb had declined, and eventually the quiet Generals had resorted to merely pilfering the inventor's notebooks after his death. A dishonorable endeavor, true, but the Fifth Empire's needs had trumped the poor judgment of Tesla.

Many years later, the Gods of Steel, Electricity, and Glass had changed the city forever; where once a mere trading town had bubbled away, the skyline now rose in towering spires of light. Asphalt covered the ground for millions of kilometers.

Fortunately, it was the kind of city that attracted those people society still considered "eccentric." If the citizenry saw a bald man in black piloting an automobile over a century old, they would smile and wave. If that same man, whilst walking through a "mall"—such a barbaric word—the kind of monosyllabic, swallowed moan that one found befitting for this current *déclassé* iteration of human existence—perhaps paused and drank an entire Orange Julius in one long swallow, nobody even noticed or cared.

There were, as was the case with any society (no matter how uncultured), shining gems in their repertoire. A chilled drink with a mixture of citrus, dairy, and egg proteins, whipped to a froth? Divine. It was easily digested by the metal vat of artificial zymogens in his belly and resulted in no waste material whatsoever. Affordably priced at the rough equivalent of a Florin or two in his youth. And quite delicious!

He wasn't the kind of person who felt a pressing need to catalogue each separate individual in a room—fortunate, as the food court was enormous. He watched the crowd in batches of five, ten, or fifteen at a time, his eyes taking in postures, body language, and quickly identifying those who didn't easily fit into a modern mall archetype.

When his gaze finally settled, it was on something red.

Not cherry or tomato, not fire engine or lipstick. This was the color of a horse-drawn carriage in Germany a hundred years before. The lacquered patina of the trim on Chinese temples when it had still been fresh. A British soldier's uniform after it had been soaked in blood in India.

And it was the color of two stripes in her hair. Not a tone you'd naturally see on a woman's head. The rest was burgundy, nothing terribly special in this day and age, striking but not as unique as the two streaks.

Not as unique as the peculiar corset and trousers of black denim and lace visible under the tattered excuse of a bustle skirt. Not as unique as the boots, which looked like they'd been stitched together from seven different time periods, two of which had yet to occur.

Also not as unique as her brass aviator's goggles, the lenses smoky. Even though he couldn't see her eyes behind them, he could tell she'd caught him staring. It was the kind of day where that could happen, blast it all, and he ducked behind an escalator as fast as possible.

WHERE DID HE *go?*
She'd had him in her sights, not figuratively, but literally tagged in the duplex crosshairs etched into her ocular reticle (an upgrade from the less reliable one of wire, damaged in the retreat from the Battle of Maiwand, which she still maintained—on the record and off—was the biggest bit of political skullduggery she'd ever seen.)

That battle had also cost her nine percent of the peripheral vision in her right eye, which was not enough to warrant a replacement but certainly enough to aggravate. She had to turn her head to scan the groups of indolent but gaily-dressed young adults and wet-nurses pushing children in fabulous perambulators. On the main floor, enormous sheets of glass safeguarded sparkling storefronts. One level above, a centrally-located gilt lift began its descent. Just behind a cart filled with smoked-glass spectacles was the mechanical staircase. Her eyes scanned beyond the whirring motors, rubber belting, and glass partitions to locate the one that spoke poetry with a single, sliding glance.

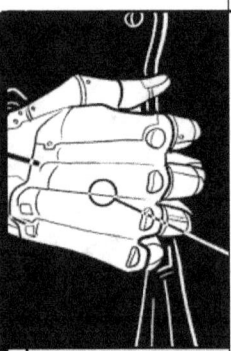

Ah! There he was, behind a teetering display of cheap scent and jewelry that would turn the skin green. The biorhythms were correct, despite the elevated pulse . . .

She swallowed.

He kept his human heart.

She thought of the years that had gone by, the upgrades he'd endured to become a Collector. How had he convinced Them to let something so weak and fragile as a human heart to remain at the center of his mechanical being?

Not that it mattered. The Company now required the retrieval of his brass memory cylinders. She licked her lips and wondered.

Wondered if he'd recognize her.

Wondered if he was going to come along quietly or if she'd have to "persuade" him.

One thing was for certain: if he ran, and forced her to chase him in these cursed boots, he'd pay for it thrice over.

OF COURSE, THIS would be the one time he'd forgotten to wind Doctor Gillenheimer's Royal Clockwork Mesmerizer, Mark IV. Of course. The damnable contraption had lain in his pocket for decades, a lump made to protect him from her kind should he ever need it, and had he ever set foot outside his flat without making sure the little brass key in its back was wound a full ten clicks? Not once, no, but that morning he'd somehow glossed over it. It was one of those kinds of days, indeed.

Running was out of the question. Any woman of her breed who wore such boots could doubtless sprint like a gazelle in them if necessary. Or, more to the point, a cheetah. A very angry cheetah in a corset.

He could attempt to wind the damned thing, but its noise would likely draw her attention even faster. Bloody useless. Doctor Gillenheimer's benefactors had poured finances into his research, paid bills that would bankrupt a sultan, in order for this little blob to exist, and it was as pointless in his hand as an Orange Julius would have been.

No, wait. He could have drunk the Orange Julius.

Not long now. Nothing to be done for it. Had he sweat glands, he'd have doubtless mopped his brow. A quick check showed everything was in order. Dress slacks, turtleneck, tuxedo jacket, leather loafers all the color of a brand-new piano. Not a speck of dirt or lint, nor a hair out of place.

A quick decision was made. He put on Smile #45 (*Greeting From A Strange Window Washer in August, 1956 in Perth at 7:16 a.m.*), ducked out from behind the escalator and thrust his hand forward in greeting.

THE ORIGINS OF the handshake are unclear, though Bascom Octavius speculated in his 19— work *The Social Rituals of the Empire* that it might have originated with Sir Lucien Osborne. It had less to do with polite salutation and everything to do with self-preservation, as Sir Lucien liked to assure himself that the man opposite wasn't holding a sword in his right hand. As Sir Lucien was renowned for his predilection for married women (and their daughters and, if rumors were correct, the prettier of the noble-born sons as well,) this practice worked out very well indeed for him until he bedded the fraternal twins of the Duke of Craighinn, who happened to be left-handed.

It also explained why most bounty hunters thought of a proffered hand as an opening to "slip a mark the Sir Lucien," but she didn't have a sword on her and, in any case, They wanted him alive, if possible. There was a brief moment in which she took in his impeccable attire—*the man always did know how to wear a dress jacket*—and the smile that threatened to undo her all over again before she had him by the wrist.

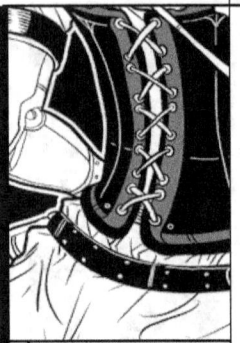

The last time I saw him in that coat, she remembered, *I still had a human heart, too.*

Over her more-practical trousers, she wore a bustled overskirt he should have recognized, but what was once virginal white silk with hand embroidery was now tattered and oil-stained. She'd dyed it black with the darkest India ink she could find, torn it apart with a pair of tiny, gold scissors, and stitched it back together with tears and curses as clockwork whirred inside her.

"You don't look the least bit surprised to see me," she told her prey as she twisted about, intending to put him on the floor for long enough to cuff him and arrange for transport. "Have you missed me, darling?"

HIS SMILE DROPPED like a handful of surprised scorpions.

"Unpreparedness is not part of my chit-cog library, and neither is desire increased by temporal longevity" he said, worrying about the grate in his tone. He hadn't oiled his vocal cables since September 8, 1963 because he so rarely used them. "But you know that, of course. I suppose you'll be wanting to wrap up these matters?"

One of the screw-records in his skull (one of the few authentic bones left in his body, a process accelerated by a terrible attack in Constantinople, 1922) ticked its needle into a groove he hadn't used since before the end of the American Civil War. Motes of dust parted as the brass spike read information long, long disused.

It was the kind of information one had to keep quiet about. Allow no outward reaction. Do not let others perceive. But in a powder-flash of inspiration, he realized there might be a way out of this mess.

"If you take my head right now, madam," he said evenly, "there will be witnesses. How many people here, do you think, can capture photographic perma-nent impressions via their aethergrammic telephone devices? And then the hunt will be called, will it not?"

HE HAD A point, bugger it all: all matters of the Empire were to be kept *sub rosa*. Though the patrons of the curious establishment had yet to take notice of her recent actions or her threat to his person, they had noted with various levels of disapproval, condemnation, appreciation, and arousal both her hair and her choice of apparel. Since entering this place, she'd been subjected to stares, cat-calls, whistles, and various offers of a dubious nature, all of which had been only moderately less appealing than the stench of food grease and the press of sloppy, imperfect humanity.

Sloppy and imperfect they may well be, but they all carried the aforementioned slim, threatening communication modules equipped with pictorial capabilities. Deactivating him in public wouldn't help matters any. One set of onlookers might preserve the moment in their curious version of a magic lantern show while the others called for the local law enforcement.

Local law enforcement never helped, in her experience, no matter the time or place.

And there was the problem with his scent. Close enough now to catch the metal-tang of his inner workings, she thought her sense-memory might have betrayed her. While this was indeed her quarry, she couldn't be absolutely certain this was the man who had left her, if not at the marriage altar then certainly close to it, more than a hundred years before. The tilt to his head, the cut of the coat might be the same, but too much of him had been replaced with machinery over the years to be sure.

I was so certain I'd found him, when They sent me the brief.

"You are going to start walking," she told him, "and not make a fuss, or I will take just your head back to Them and apologize for leaving the rest of you folded in a heap in Housewares."

"VERY WELL," HE said, and chose another smile (*Prim Closed Mouth #14: occidental lady in train to Peking, 1908*). He bowed at the waist, just a fraction of an inch, then proffered his right arm in a most proper manner. "Angelus A. Morphew, at your service."

A glass bead the size of a printed period fell into its tiny hole in his chest. Four more holes, four more little beads awaited. Lies were not becoming of a true gentleman, not even lily-white ones, and he'd agreed to Doctor Gillenheimer's Weighted Miniature Artificial Morality Tabulator Mark III without any real fuss. He made a note to check its calibration—his *nom de guerre* should not have registered as a mistruth.

She stared at him in a manner that caused another disused part of his workings to tick into action for the first time in countless ages. Truly, this one was a formidable opponent; her mere presence gave his internals a more thorough congruity check than any in even the most austere German labs ever had.

"My apologies," he said after a half-second's pause. "We have met before, yes? You will understand if I do not recall. As a man you may be acquainted with once said, *Zwar weiß ich viel, doch möchte ich mehr wissen.*"

"ES MUß SICH *erst noch zeigen*," she retorted, the brass German-translator punch card having slid into the correct slot without so much as a by-her-leave, "if you don't mind my saying so... Herr Morphew."

She didn't owe him the courtesy of using a human title; he was at least seventy-five percent mechanical or she wouldn't be here. Yet she took his arm as though they were about to enter a dim Victorian parlor, or the Grand Ballroom at Neuschwanstein. It made sense, primarily because she wanted to keep him close and there were several lovely pressure points along the inner arm that she could use, if necessary, to interrupt his artificial bloodflow.

Her boots also pinched her toes, and it was nice to lean on someone for a change.

Fatigue clambered up her skirts with cold fingers, trying to pull her back into a near-coma that would allow her inner workings to run a diagnostic. Shifting always took it right out of her, but this time was different.

Tick . . . tick . . . tick . . .

Her heart's tiny balance springs and staffs, regulators and wheels had already slowed to a near-standstill. She bit the inside of her cheek and tried to figure out what the hell was happening, because she shouldn't have been synching to match Morphew's leisurely and debonair —and human—pulse. Still, now wasn't the time for the cheap theatrics of a ladylike swoon.

"Corentine Reilly," she said as they headed to the double doors at the front of the store. "Collector Retrieval Squad, Division 3. Please do me the courtesy of accompanying me somewhere more secluded and appropriate to continue this conversation."

"A PLEASURE," HE said as another glass bead slipped into its appropriate hole.

They were seventeen steps from a large pair of double glass doors. Once upon a time, he would have categorized the style of such a portal—*Classical Revival, Second Empire, Italianate*—but society had eschewed such details for decades, favoring now these artless, flat structures with no real spirit or craft in their manufacture. Rectangles set in bland steel or, heaven forbid, aluminum.

The needle barely ticked over a simple line in its read cylinder: *May 9th, 1988, Costa Mesa*—this portion has been reallocated. Nothing remained of what had once

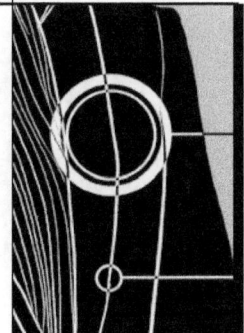

been a hefty collection of brass data records regarding architectural style. They'd been wiped clean, then grooved again in order to accompany his growing need for more space on Observation and Investigation No. 644-J-92.

His investigation had been ongoing for long enough that many other segments of brass had been marked with the same note. His head could only carry a finite amount of blanks. Sometimes he wondered what he'd overwritten.

Nothing too important.

"I must confess," he began, and stopped. She turned to him and waited, the lenses of her goggles reflecting his own visage in tandem, a shrunken version of his face. A gaggle of teenagers in bright colors parted around them (giggling over some crass and impolite joke, no doubt). "Many are the rumors that fly about your branch of the Company, madam. Perhaps you will find me an easier companion if you would be kind enough to answer a few questions?"

Her head inclined after a moment. Not an explicit nod, but he took what little succor he could and barreled ahead.

"Is the Fifth Empire truly coming to an end? Have collectors of information, such as myself, been relegated to the Great and Terrible Warehouses in favor of silicon and plastic constructs?"

ONE OF THE teenagers jostled her roughly; his various belts, chains and piercings clanked and jingled like a sleigh.

Or a Russian troika. Nestled in furs and surrounded by snow, they skimmed the surface of the world gone silent, save for the bells that announced their presence. Two of the horses always turned to look back at the past year, and the center looked ahead to the unknown future. She-who-would-be-Corentine had laughed at the idea that tomorrow held anything but possibilities.

But that was long ago, and that Empire had collapsed and burned as so many of the others before it. Now the Fifth Empire was at a close, and They wanted the information imprinted on the cylinders: documentation that would be used to forge the success of the Rising Sixth.

"Yes," she said shortly. "And that is the only answer you'll get from me. For now. This is no fairy tale. There are no riddles three."

She took another step, but was held fast by the vice of his arm, which pinned hers against his side. Rough conversations, the sounds of filthy lucre changing hands, the wail of a despondent infant couldn't quite mask the whirring in Corentine's ears as she glared at him.

"I suggest, very firmly, that you start moving."

With her free hand, she shoved her goggles atop her head. Very few of the Collectors ever looked into Corentine Reilly's eyes and survived to resist. The Council classified them as a the same shade as a variety of the mineral beryl $(Be3Al2(SiO3)6,)$ colored green by trace amounts of chromium and vanadium. Poets had called them emerald pools and other such nonsense. Corentine simply thought of them as a primary weapon against recalcitrant males, and though they were not physically equipped to shoot sparks, she nevertheless leveled a very narrow look at him.

MUCH LIKE A stream suddenly branching in two directions, Read Needle 16c came to a fork in one of the grooves in his head. The counterbalance weight shifted it to the left side, and a long-abandoned stream of words floated up out of cold, metallic sleep:

I shall remain, watching all earth and sky;
The house of my heart can be seen in
    your eye;
A bloodless heart you keep;
And emerald eyes shan't we—

CURRENT FUGITIVE ALIAS/OPERATING NAME

ANGELUS A. MORPHEW

COMPANY STATUS	OPERATING NUMBER
AT LARGE	#1-17B

STANDARD BRASS CONSTRUCTION MEMORY CYLINDER ASSEMBLY.

NEEDLE-ACCESSED BRASS PLATENS; MERCURY VALVE AND COG ASSISTED DRIVES. ["SCREW DRIVES"]

SUB DERMAL FACIAL PLATE ASSEMBLY [SKIN REMOVED TO SHOW DETAIL]

SMILE # 45

VOICE SIMULATION VOCAL CABLES

NOTED: BIOLOGICAL HUMAN HEART STILL ACTIVE, SUPPLEMENTED WITH ARTIFICIAL BLOODFLOW REGULATORS AND PUMPING FLUID 7A MAGNESANGUE.

INSTALLED: DOCTOR GILLENHEIMER'S WEIGHTED MINIATURE MORALITY TABULATOR: MARK III

STOMACH PROCESSING ASSEMBLY [ARTIFICIAL ZYMOGEN BASE]

CARRIED IN POCKET: DOCTOR GILLENHEIMER'S ROYAL CLOCKWORK MESMERIZER, MARK IV

MECHANICALLY ENHANCED HAND AND FINGER ASSEMBLY [SKIN COVERING REMOVED TO SHOW DETAILS]

SCHEMATICS RENDERED BY MR. PAUL SIZER, IN THE YEAR 2010

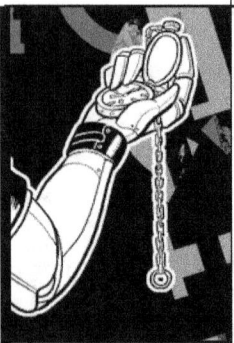

The needle skipped as it broadsided another information track, jumped into a reset groove, and finished. Peculiar, but it was a peculiar kind of day, and, he begrudgingly noted, quite possibly his last. The last time such a snippet had occurred was for a similar misread error: old information, improperly blanked and rewritten upon.

He could not shake the feeling this one's eyes had something to do with it. They were beautifully constructed, even when her micro-servos were held at a perfect position to project the possibility of imminent doom.

"Onward, then. In lieu of information, I would beg a boon of you, madam." He stepped toward the door, uncomfortably aware that she remained close enough to strike if he moved so much as a millimeter toward freedom. "It appears that I have always known that my time upon this, aha, mortal coil would be finite. My brass has been rewritten and blanked so many times that I no longer recall when I was born, nor my original mission."

They continued along the sidewalk, and each step lowered his odds of survival dramatically. The end was likely nigh by forty-eight point two percent and rising, plus or minus two-thousandths of a percent.

He'd never calculated it as above thirteen point four percent. Not even when a mad Cossack had smashed his skull with a rifle butt.

"It has been ages since even a true and proper shop in the service of the Empire has seen my workings. Many of my replacements and internal repairs have been done myself. You can imagine my surprise," he said as they marched past rows of motor carriages (ugly plastic and vinyl, *vinyl*, of all the blasphemies mankind could dream up—slick and disgustingly malleable and incapable of storing a proper record for more than a day, but shreds of it

remained and lingered for thousands of years in the soil as offal), "when a recent repair of my left temporal aft section, directly behind the ear, yielded a very small scroll wrapped in a scarlet ribbon. Very small writing, in my own hand it seems. I refrained from peeking, but, well . . . it seems to have been there for quite some time, and the placement makes one think it was to be delivered in the event of my demise. Only barest scratches remain in my banks regarding the person it's addressed to; all I know is that we met in the Russian town of Dobryanka. Would you . . . *could* you please see that this final message is delivered?"

He paused, suddenly aware that they'd turned a corner. The back end of a Dillard's would be, it seemed, his final destination. He'd never understood the shop itself: ridiculous clothing for men and women, the kind that even wanton strumpets of the *Bois de Boulogne* would never have worn.

Sixty-eight point eight percent, and rising. It was time.

"Please? The scroll is addressed to someone named Annabelle."

SHE SLAMMED HIM into the brick wall, ignoring the rubbish and noisome puddles that dotted the alleyway. Forearm braced against his windpipe, she leaned forward to hiss at him like a snake.

"And what do those barest scratches on your memory banks say, Angelus A. Morphew? Do you remember what this Annabelle looked like? Where she came from? What she was doing in a god-forsaken place like the *Permsky Kray* with someone like you?"

He didn't answer, and so Corentine shoved harder, pressing against the unyielding metal plates that covered the masculine-form of the Collector's body.

"Maybe if I open your panels and stir the metal mess you call a brain, those cylinders of yours will yield better answers.

A judicious application of electrical current might also help loosen your tongue."

As she leaned in—a passerby might have mistaken the gesture as part of a romantic but ill-advised tryst in the dank and narrow corridor between buildings—her right hand slid behind his ear and she extracted the scroll.

Her clockwork heart seized, and for a moment Corentine thought she might remain frozen for all time, trapped in a suit of moldering flesh that would fall away from her, one rotten chunk at a time, until all that was left were upgrades of brass and copper.

She'd almost convinced herself she'd been mistaken, almost convinced herself that he was merely a ghost come to haunt her, to remonstrate, to torture, and condemn. She didn't know what was written on the scroll, but the blood-red ribbon that bound it had been hers once upon another time, and the scent-memory attached to it was so strong that she wanted to stagger back, to be sick all over the already filthy pavement.

Instead, she held fast to the steel in her spine and scanned his face, so different than the one she remembered, the eyes that had been extracted and replaced with glass orbs, the carefully-blank expression.

"By all the hells, what did They do to you?"

The needles plucked away from the brass and, as one, they hovered on the outer edges of their respective cylinders. A visiting spider might have heard their ghostly ticks as they sought and found remnant lines outside of the main information tracks.

charlatans. One needn't visit a séance to find

Some were only endings.

once was a thriving port, but the advent of the locomotive has rendered it an abandoned shell.

Others only beginnings:

Should you ever find yourself reading this information, then the game has finally run its course . . .

That one stopped his mechanisms. It appeared to be a full groove, complete and whole, but none of the mercury valves or cogs showed that he'd ever accessed it. The needle lowered again.

. . . run its course. As you well know, old chap, the ages have required rather many instances of blanking these copper plates and brass cylinders. Please do trust yourself. Nothing that has been written over was necessary information. On the contrary, it was extraneous and often worthless. Only on a few occasions have you erased anything you might have kept elsewhere, but due to immediate need you chose to heat the grooves and smooth them to nothingness. There is a message in your cranial cavities that will tie up the only loose thread, should you perish, and that one . . . that one was blanked to spare you a life of suffering and regret, of heartache and loss. You are better off not knowing. Whoever your attacker may be, do all within your power to encourage their hand. Tally ho, sire, and may a flight of angels sing thee to thy well deserved rest. Vivat Regnum!

So.

The pressure on his throat lessened enough to work the vocal cables once more. There was no time for sadness. There never had been, not once that he was aware of. If this proved to be the final curtain, he would take a bow gracefully.

"I am a traitor to the Empire," he said. "I have abetted our enemies, and have betrayed you all."

Deep in his chest, two glass beads fell into their holes.

CORENTINE THOUGHT SHE heard something, like two raindrops hitting a tin

roof, but the sound was as small as their chances of seeing the next dawn.

"I hate to remind you," she told him, "but you never could successfully lie to me. Traitor to the Empire, my arse. You can't even remember your real name, so save the programmed message of humble servility for someone who'll buy it."

As much as she wanted to untie the scroll and read it this instant, she knew They'd be coming soon. The sensors would tell Them that she'd had the Collector in her possession and she'd made the decision not to deactivate, not to transport. Corentine cursed, fluently, in six languages, switching between them as needed to achieve maximum effect, and took a step back.

As she did so, her watch whirred in protest. She reached for the Company-issued timepiece, a lovely thing of gold and glint, and opened it. How many times had she used it to summon a portal? How many times had she sent metal men and women back, their cylinders destined for harvest and the rest for the scrap and smelting?

The inscription caught her eye: *Commune bonum.*

Corentine let the watch dangle by its chain. It caught the fading sunlight and reflected it onto the Collector's face until she dropped it into the muck and used the heel of her boot to break it to smithereens. She thought of just what they could do with their "common good" and exactly where they could stick it as she exhaled.

"We need to start moving. They're going to send someone else, and I'd rather not make the chase an easy one."

He didn't answer right away, didn't so much as twitch to indicate a hidden cylinder rotating slowly, committing her treason to brass memory.

DAMNATION. HIS RUSE hadn't worked.

There was more than one method of beating the soot from a rug. His information banks were aware of thirty-nine. An even fifty if you counted the direction of each strike.

"It seenks," he said, then held up a hand to beg a pause. Using both thumbs, he popped the dent out of his windpipe. A noise like a fisherman's reel spinning out too fast came and went as he cleared the kinks from his throat cables and then tried again.

Fifty-five percent and . . . falling? Several needles stopped, lifted, reversed their read direction and descended back to the copper.

"It seems that there is more to your life than mere collection, madam." He gestured toward a horseless carriage far to their right. Although very few in the mall would have identified it due to its perceived "old age," he still viewed it as a beautiful new form of transport: a black Rolls Royce V8. One of only three made in secret for members of the Fifth in 1906.

He'd never had the heart to abandon or modify it.

"I know not why you would shirk your duties, nor what could inspire you to halt a perfectly viable collection. Chance is an amusing mistress at times. My chariot awaits."

The thimble-sized scrap of fatty tissue in his head, all that remained of his original "manufacture," as he sometimes considered it, did not understand the feeling whirring through his mind. None of his brass indices or vacuum-sealed quicksilver microtubes contained any relevant entries on it either. He cross referenced, jimmied a cog or two, and spun some gears in puzzlement at the nearest description he could find, and finally made a new entry on platen 17a, line 34:

Hope.

SHE APPRECIATED THE motor car, as much for the old leather and clean lines as the chance to rest her feet. Once inside, she felt the balance of power shift: his vehicle, his city, his hands at the wheel. She didn't know where he was headed or what awaited them upon arrival. Perhaps he only bided his time and still planned to make a run for it. Perhaps he'd serve her tea and cakes laced with cyanide; she was still human enough to succumb to poison, never mind suffocation, shooting, stabbing, and the like.

Corentine had survived such attacks before, but only with the aid of the Company's pocket watch. She'd shifted back to headquarters, bleeding and battered, more than a dozen times in her career. Attacks on her person accounted for several curious scars, a metal plate or two . . .

But the clockwork heart was my own fault.

Or his.

So if he chose to wrap those same, metal-reinforced hands about her neck and squeeze, there was no watch to whisk her back, no team of doctors that would safeguard her existence. She'd gone rogue, and she was as good as dead anyway. Appropriate that her life would be counted off in the number of seconds, minutes, hours, even though the pocket watch lay in a pile of broken bits of balance wheels and busted mainspring.

"It's very freeing," she told her reflection in the window, "to know that death is once again a possibility."

If she was going to die soon, she'd better hurry and read the contents of the mysterious scroll.

What will it be, do you think? A letter of farewell? And admission of guilt? An explanation as to why he didn't come for me as promised?

It didn't matter that he'd missed their rendezvous all those years ago, just as it didn't matter that she'd destroyed the watch; if it took Them seconds or minutes, hours or days, They would chase the missing Collector and the rogue Retriever until all that was metal on this earth rusted and crumbled. They were as good as dismantled.

The bit of silk that bound it was nearly threadbare, and yet the colour glowed against her skin like blood-on-snow.

"This ribbon was once mine. My guess is that you blanked your memory cylinders . . ." *The ones I was sent to retrieve . . .* "at some time long-past." She swallowed hard and tasted zinc and nickel at the back of her throat. "I'm sure you had something much more important to record."

A SCARLET STORM was rising. If he did not hurry to his abode, they would both perish under the grasping fingers of those who plucked the marionette strings of whatever new order had come.

"Madam . . . Mistress Corentine," he said, and reactive wires in his skull activated a sense of shame over his lack of formality. "I know not entirely of which you speak. There is a familiarity here. I will neither deny nor dodge it."

He smiled again, this time choosing an analogue that reflected his own feelings: *Dying infantryman, Armenia, 1917.*

"My curiosity threatens to disobey its programming." He applied the brake at an oncoming traffic light (*lantern*, his mind insisted, but he'd learned to ignore such shallow grooves in his platens). "How did I acquire your ribbon? Have you and I danced together in the great courtyards of the Empire?"

"WE DID MORE than dance," she said as they idled at a stoplight. The area was secluded, the red light that halted them a feeble sentinel against the approaching dark. Corentine didn't need a useless lump of flesh in her chest to hate the personage sitting alongside her, so debonairly inquiring as to their shared history. "I was called Annabelle then."

The light turned green. Someone in a plastic automobile behind them honked impatiently. Angelus applied the accelerator, and they were off once again.

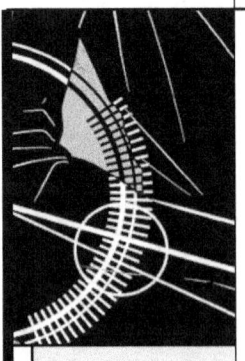

She unrolled the scroll and handed it to him, not caring that they were yet to a secured location and even less that it would mean nothing to him.

"Read that out loud, for the sake of edification, and don't mind if I bask in the knowledge that it will all be recorded on one of your damned brass cylinders again."

READING PAPERWORK WHILE hurtling along at one hundred and twenty kilometers per hour, no matter what, was not an acceptable situation. He came to a decision quickly and pulled the car over while gently depressing the brake. Rubber tires crunched into gravel, sending tiny stones up to nick the flawless paint of his vehicle. Once they'd come to a complete stop, he killed the engine and respectfully took the paper from her hand.

"Very well," he said, and gave her a patient smile (*Ticket Clerk, Zeppelin Station, Gdansk, 1914*). His first glance told him it was a tiny thing, this piece of paper that was the color of old honey with ink faded to lavender over the ages. Each letter was miniscule, the size of a printed period, really, and no ordinary human being would have seen more than tiny clusters of dots.

His ocular focus sprockets ticked over with the sounds of grasshoppers cracking their knuckles, and his field of vision narrowed. The letters leapt to life then, and flowed through his mind as linen would beneath a seamstress's machine, spilling from his tongue as faery gold spills from the hands of those who attempt to grasp it upon waking:

My dearest Annabelle,
While you sleep a mere ten meters away in the guest suite of Baron Krausmeyer's haus, I write these things to you under mine own hand, one of the few parcels of flesh I can still claim are genuine.
A week ago I received new orders, and that is why tonight I shall embark upon a voyage to America. Along the way I shall be augmented in several new ways. You know too well the wound that has plagued me since the Russian incident. They shall remove my damaged caudate nucleus and replace it with another of Dr. G_____'s great works. I am assured that the replacement will allow greater function than the failing flesh God hath imbued us all with.
When my operation is complete, I shall never be able to love again. Norepinephrine and dopamine hath no purchase upon brass and copper. All I have felt for you, every moment I have gazed into your eyes and believed I found paradise, every sweet kiss or moment we stole behind our superiors' backs shall be for naught. Love shall die, for me.
I would not subject you to the same terrible future.
This morning, I was the last thing you gazed upon with human eyes. Would that I could have been brave enough to refuse your request, but you proved your valor, and the Empire's doctors conceded to your demands for the operation. I came and held your hand as they gave you the gases to lull you into the realm of Morpheus.
When you open your beautiful eyelids, those eyes will not be flesh, and I shall not remain.
Cowardly, indeed. Had I other recourse, please, I beg thee, know that I would have taken it.
Weep if you must and hate me if it will speed your recovery. I am quickly becoming more construct than corpus, more machine than man. You are still mostly flesh. Your eyes and left hand are your only augmentations. Your heart still beats blood, whereas I am quickly becoming a mere copper golem with oil in his veins. Annabelle deserves better. You will find it, I have no fear, for you are young, and I do believe they shall transfer you to another department soon. Your affinity for numbers makes you prime Sergeant material. You will find another, a man

who can love and cherish you as I will no longer be able. Perhaps, provided enough of your sweet body is allowed to remain intact, you shall bear many sons for the Empire.

I shall always strive to keep my heart, hands, and eyes as human as they are this very day. It is a silly belief, the pale hope of a doomed man facing his greatest storm, but perchance a tiny part of what I feel this night will live on in my heart. Perchance my fingertips will remember the softness of your skin, or my eyes will give dreams of the ghost of you in visions.

Live, love, heal and be strong for the continuance of Man's Greatest Hope. If you read this, know I died having loved you. I could not have asked for more.

Forever yours,
A. A. M.

The automobile's engine had stopped its tinny pings and ticks by the time the last word faded from his lips.

THE COMPANY'S DAMNED motto echoed in the silence that spiraled out between them as the voices of the past faded. *Commune bonum.* The Common Good. They used such words in their speeches, on their posters, in the printed material distributed in schools in conjunction with words like *valor* and *honor* and *for the glory of the Empire!* . . . words war-tattered about the edges and stained with tears. Vomit. Blood.

Such words lured children onto the battlefield and wrapped their battered, broken bodies in a winding-sheet for transport home to weeping families. Such words were thin consolation, rough with all the things left unsaid. Such words were diamonds dangled before starry-eyed girls, to whom honor and glory were jewels beyond compare, brighter than circlets of gold slipped upon a willing finger.

She'd been just such a girl. She'd been just such a fool, thinking that they would work for the greater good and the glory of the Empire hand in mechanical hand.

"It reads like a note of farewell. But I—Annabelle—never got it. Mischance or misdeed, it doesn't really matter now."

Corentine twined the red ribbon through her fingers and remembered all the times she'd worn it: climbing the Pyrénées, subverting His Majesty's Bodyguard of the Honourable Corps of Gentlemen at Arms long enough to poison a monarch; walking along the rocky beaches of the Cherno More, whose waters were not exactly black, but still dark, with the floor unfathomable. Corentine knew, now, that the water's hydrogen sulfide layer supported a unique microbial population, producing black sediments most likely due to anaerobic methane oxidation, but she preferred to think of the darkness as secrets.

Though the muscle was gone, useless poetic longings lingered. The irony!

"When I realized you'd gone, I had Them take my heart. Cowardice for cowardice; the pain of you leaving was greater than anything They could have done to me." Not an accusation, not said to hurt, for she doubted there was enough of him left to wound with words. But the simple truth was a sword she used to remonstrate herself. "I tried . . . days, I think. Maybe months. But every second you were gone was like the second-hand on a clock ticking over, and it somehow consoled me to mark your absence by the seconds, by the hours."

She could have told him, only a few hours ago, just how many seconds had passed since last she'd seen him. But Time had dilated the moment she'd spotted him in the crowd. Corentine recalled a wild-haired German that had shouted at her at length about relativity, but she'd never truly understood until her internal clockwork synched to the man of metal sitting so still alongside her.

His inner mechanisms whirred along, undeterred, while hers slowed almost to a standstill and then reset to mark their time together, however brief that might be.

One. Two. Three...

Corentine lifted the ribbon and tied it into her hair, where she knew the jaunty, incongruent bow would burn against the burgundy and black. Perhaps the next Agent of the Empire would train his weapon on the bright flower of color and put a bullet in her head.

But her heart would tick on, wouldn't it?

Fourteen . . . fifteen . . . sixteen . . .

"It seemed like the right thing to do at the time, and They were only too willing to experiment on me. I thought it would be a relief, but it wasn't. Hand, heart, eyes; the things they took, that I gave up readily. Your note says you'd keep them, but I see you didn't quite manage it."

THE SKIN OF his fingers resembled the parchment of the scroll in many ways. He gently rolled the message back into its original shape and cradled it in his palm, where the gentle breeze rocked it to and fro by several millimeters.

"There are two entries in my frontal cores that state that I must not replace my heart or hands or eyes. I have sometimes wondered why I'd committed them to memory."

Her own eyes were polished ivory inlays set with carefully camouflaged lenses. Some mad artist had gone to the trouble of painting filament veins in the corners, each the size of the hair on a honeybee's leg. He smiled at her again momentarily (*Matchstick girl on the streets of Oslo, December 1889*).

"I have dreamed, madam. The laboratories took so much of me, but I have experienced dreams every night, regardless of my augmentations. In some, a woman such as yourself laughs as snow falls all around us. With all that has happened today, I do believe that you and I loved once. If my banks are to be believed, I most likely loved you without reservation. Such an odd existence this is."

He reached forward, slowly, carefully, and offered her his hand. Whoever had done the work on her replacement surface had been brilliant; her new fingers were warm to the touch and soft as fine silk. Only their strong, calculated grip belied the artifice inherent.

"We are about to be intercepted," he said, as a high-pitched tintinnabulation increased in volume. "They say that collection is a painless process. However, should you desire, I will fight them alongside you . . . ?"

He left the question hanging in the air.

SHE HELD HIS hand in hers, feeling the pseudo-pulse of Fluid 7A MagneSangue through his arterial corridors. The noise was getting louder now; wind rocked the vintage automobile and sought its way through every crevice in glass and steel.

"How long do we have?" he asked.

"A minute. Maybe less." She didn't know what she expected: a glimmer of fear, a surge of adrenaline, but he only blinked as processors shifted, calculated . . .

Counted down.

There wasn't enough of him left to feel anything; not fear, not remorse. Even the offer to stand and fight was born out of ages-old algorithms designed to simulate fight-or-flight responses. They did have to protect themselves, their documentation, until the appropriate representative to arrive to collect. The offer was a hollow one, an echo of shades past, of times when they'd stood back-to-back, swords in hand and pistols drawn. Perhaps somewhere, buried deep inside him, a blanked cylinder retained enough information to recall the time they'd fought their way out of the Citadella atop Gellért Hill.

Hard to forget Budapest, even without the cannon fire aimed our direction and a

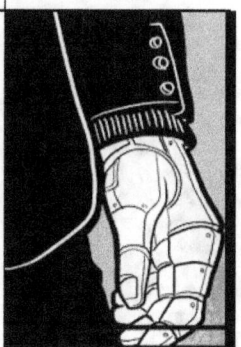

hundred foot-soldiers dogging us to the border.

We were both different people then.

Corentine brought his hand to her cheek, wishing desperately that it smelled of gunpowder, cologne, blood, sweat, shit; anything. But there were only thin traces of the alloys that comprised his entire being.

The portal was fully open now. Less than twenty seconds remained.

Her words spoke themselves. "Do you still love me?"

They both heard the last glass bead fall, pinging in his chest as he answered.

"Yes."

Sound category: *A child's marble dancing down the hot pavement, Brooklyn, Summer, 1909.*

CORENTINE LEFT INTERROGATION Room #14 with the barest of sighs. An arduous process, trying to explain the destruction of her pocket watch, first to her immediate supervisors and then the Review Board. Harder still to explain the total destruction of #1-17B's brass cylinders. One hundred and fifty years of documentation lost. Such a thing had not happened in the entire history of the Company.

A freak accident, of course. Memory modules had never before suffered such an explosion, forceful enough to destroy a Retriever's fingers. A pristine track record and exemplary conduct in a thousand improbably difficult situations had also bought her quite a lot of benefit of the doubt.

—brass cylinders comprised of older alloys and therefore vulnerable during the Shift.

Possible sabotage implanted by #1-17b.

The Retriever did her best to preserve the materials and suffered the loss of her hands.

Please fill out Requisitions Order 57-TP. The cost of a replacement timepiece will be docked from your wages.

Recommendation: 30 days leave with pay and secondary-level review after release from the Medical Center.

The attachment points for her replacement hands were nearly healed, but the scar on her chest would take longer. Corentine's new heart skipped a beat, unaccustomed as yet to its new surroundings. Perhaps a step backwards into sloppy humanity, but it would have been a waste to leave it there.

The last message, the one he couldn't read, had spewed forth from his frontal lobe as Doctor Gillenheimer's Weighted Miniature Artificial Morality Tabulator Mark III shut him down for exceeding acceptable limits for falsehoods:

"I kept my heart, because it was not mine to give away. It's always belonged to you."

Such a funny word, "always."

I'll always count off the seconds until we meet in the next world, my love.

Corentine nodded, then adjusted the ribbon-bow in her hair, the one that reminded everyone who met her of a blood-flower in full bloom. ❧

James L. Grant is best known as the artist half of the duo that creates *Two Lumps*, a cartoon about cats. Just to prove that he can do more than doodle, his funky fiction has appeared in various magazines in the last six years, and he has sold two novels. He is currently living in Dallas, Texas, with his wife and co-creator, Mel Hynes, and working on selling his third novel.

Lisa Mantchev is the author of *Eyes Like Stars* and the forthcoming *Perchance To Dream*, the first two novels in the Théâtre Illuminata series. She has also published numerous short stories in venues including *Strange Horizons*, *Fantasy*, *Clarkesworld*, and *Weird Tales*. She lives on the Olympic Peninsula of Washington state with her husband, daughter, and hairy miscreant dogs.

Lost in Lovecraft

A GUIDED TOUR OF THE DARK MASTER'S WORLD

BY KENNETH HITE

> "*It is always a relief to get clear of the place, and to follow the narrow road around the base of the hills and across the level country beyond till it rejoins the Aylesbury pike. Afterwards one sometimes learns that one has been through Dunwich.*"
>
> —H.P. LOVECRAFT,
> "THE DUNWICH HORROR"

Lovecraftian critical opinion, in the persons of S.T. Joshi and his school, are as relieved as Lovecraft's narrator to "get clear of" Dunwich. Here, worse than any invisible monster, lie the seeds of August Derleth's "Derlethifying" of the Lovecraft Mythos—that is, shaping it into a battle between good and evil fought for the lives of humanity. But Lovecraft went through Dunwich for a reason, little as his soi-disant acolytes may like it. Even if "The Dunwich Horror" is, as its great introductory line has it, "the wrong fork at the junction," Lovecraft didn't take it by accident. He was led there by the call of Pan.

> "'*Inbreeding?' Armitage muttered half-aloud to himself. 'Great God, what simpletons! Shew them Arthur Machen's Great God Pan and they'll think it a common Dunwich scandal!'*"
>
> —H.P. LOVECRAFT,
> "THE DUNWICH HORROR"

Lovecraft first read British horrorist Arthur Machen in 1923, and was smitten. Over the next few years, he worked Machen's territory of hidden races, underground decadence, and invisible monsters as sedulously as he had previously explored Poe's hysterics or Dunsany's daydreams. HPL wrote "The Rats in the Walls," "The Unnamable," and "The Festival" in 1923, and Machen's tropes echo through "The Horror at Red Hook" (1925), "Cool Air" (1926), and "Pickman's

IN A DUNWICH MINUTE

Model" (1926). "The Colour Out of Space" (1927) is a Lovecraftian nihilist negative of Machen's "The Great Return," while sharing the indirectness of Machen's "The White People" and the strange wasting death from Machen's "Novel of the White Powder."

But with "The Dunwich Horror" (1928) Lovecraft went all in, composing a fugue on Machen's "The Great God Pan." "Pan" concerns an invisible god breeding with a human woman, and the defeat of the dangerous, soulless offspring therefrom. But Lovecraft builds Dunwich with more than one Machen blueprint. Machen's "Novel of the Black Seal" also features inhuman miscegenation, and the grotesque death of its spawn (complete with "slimy, wavering tentacle"!) who, like Wilbur Whateley, is "goatish." Finally, "The White People" features the diary of a child-initiate into the Aklo letters and the Voor, as well as offering that meditation on the unnatural as "sinful" that uncharacteristically animates Lovecraft's inverted Gospel story. (But reparse Machen's "attempt to penetrate into another and higher sphere in a forbidden manner" through Lovecraft's fears of contamination, and the distance closes somewhat.) Robert M. Price's thesis convinces: with "The Dunwich Horror," Lovecraft was "Derlethifying" Arthur Machen—taking a mélange of great works by a senior horrorist and blending them into something shadowed by his own concerns.

> "*Some say they've seen the gas. I heard a man living in Dunwich saw it one night like a black cloud with sparks of fire in it floating over the tops of the trees by Dunwich Common.*"
>
> —ARTHUR MACHEN,
> "THE TERROR"

Lovecraft likely got the name "Dunwich" from Machen, who used it in *The Terror,* a novel of Nature

going mad and taking its revenge upon decadent mankind. (Sound familiar?) Machen may have meant the actual town of Dunwich, in Suffolk, which more resembles Lovecraft's Innsmouth: following a century's worth of great storms, much of the town subsided into the sea. By the mid-19th century its picturesque ruins attracted tourists like H. Rider Haggard, Edward Fitzgerald, and Lovecraft's favorite modern poet, Algernon Swinburne. Lovecraft's copy of Swinburne included his poem about Dunwich, "By the North Sea." However, Swinburne never mentions Dunwich in the poem, and Lovecraft may have created the name by back-formation from "Greenwich" or the like. The "dun" town would be the dreary, faded town—a more than adequate description, with echoes of the monstrous, portentous "dun cow" of Shropshire folklore.

"Similarly, there is no 'Dunwich'—the place being a vague echo of the decadent Massachusetts countryside around Springfield—say Wilbraham, Monson, and Hampden."

—H.P. LOVECRAFT, LETTER TO AUGUST DERLETH (NOV. 6, 1931)

Lovecraft clearly based his fictional Dunwich on a congeries of real towns in south-central Massachusetts: Wilbraham, Monson, and Hampden, as he mentions above. He visited them for a week before writing the story, and soaked up local topography and folklore (including legends about spooky whippoorwills) to be reused. He moved Wilbraham north and east, to the region of Athol (where Lovecraft picked up names like Bishop and Frye, as well as the Bear's Den and Sentinel Elm Farm), into his north-Massachusetts Miskatonic Valley. Here, as Will Murray points out, was the town of (a-ha!) Greenwich, Massachusetts, doomed to drown (like the Suffolk Dunwich) under the Quabbin Reservoir, as mentioned in "The Colour Out of Space."

"It was like its father—and most of it has gone back to him in some vague realm or dimension outside our material universe; some vague abyss out of which only the most accursed rites of human blasphemy could ever have called him for a moment on the hills."

—H.P. LOVECRAFT,
"THE DUNWICH HORROR"

But more importantly than where, *what* is Lovecraft's Dunwich? Since, unlike Arkham, the town only appears in one tale, we can't separate the setting from the story, which Lovecraft structures as a parodic Gospel. Both Wilbur and the Horror are Christ-figures. Indeed, like the Castor and Pollux of Greek myth or the divine and material Christs of Gnostic heresy, both Wilbur and the Horror are, as Donald Burleson points out, twin halves of the same hero, with two natures: visible and invisible, god and man. The Horror-hero is explicitly Christological—conceived by an infinite god, born of a virgin on a corner of the year, prodigiously learned at a young age, prophesied over, emerged from a backwater to challenge the priests of the Old Law. He dies like Dionysus or Osiris (torn to shreds by wild beasts) and like Christ (on a hilltop calling for his Father)—and like them both, he will return when the End Times come. ("After summer is winter and after winter summer.")

This makes the town of Dunwich, in turn, a parody of Bethlehem, Nazareth, and Jerusalem. Like Bethlehem, Dunwich is the ancestral seat of the (un)holy lineage both of the Whateleys (fled from Salem in 1692) and of Yog-Sothoth. Here, too, the birth of the man-god is heralded by portents, though Lovecraft inverts the Star in the sky to noises under the earth. The Nazareth parallel is mostly one of common rustication, although Nathanael's query in John 1:46—"Can anything good come out of Nazareth?"—seems apropos, and Wilbur does a lot of carpentry while rebuilding the barn for his twin. Finally, the Horror dies on the hill outside Dunwich, just as Christ died on the hill outside Jerusalem—reminding us that Dunwich was founded by refugees from Salem, making Dunwich a kind of "New Salem" or "New Jerusalem."

"Straight on I walked, while all the night
Grew pale with phosphorescent light,
And wall and farmhouse gable glowed
Unearthly by the climbing road.
There was the milestone that I knew—
'Two miles to Dunwich'—now the view…"

—H.P. LOVECRAFT,
"THE ANCIENT TRACK"

One final Biblical parallel, sanctified by another great horrorist: Dunwich is Chorazin, the hamlet cursed by Christ, the

In Dunwich as in Bethlehem, the birth of the man-god is heralded by portents, though Lovecraft inverts the Star in the sky to noises under the earth.

future birthplace of the Antichrist. M.R. James' "Count Magnus" makes the "Black Pilgrimage to Chorazin," at which Lovecraft's ears must have twitched. Lovecraft gets it both ways: Christ cursed Chorazin for rejecting him just as the Dunwich folk rejected the Horror, while casting the Horror as explicit Antichrist works on the "Machen level" of sin and retribution so strangely prominent in this tale. But where Chorazin births the coming apocalypse, Dunwich is but a symptom, or better yet a preview. Dunwich is degeneration before the apocalypse; it is indeed the degeneration before the degeneration. Lovecraft uses it in much that way in his 1929 poem "The Ancient Track," the only other place where Dunwich appears in his works. That narrator, anticipating a joyous homecoming, sees the signpost for Dunwich; immediately thereafter he finds himself in "a valley of the lost and dead." Note that in the tale, the signs to Dunwich have all been taken down, and one finds Dunwich only by taking "the wrong fork at the junction of Aylesbury Pike."

The signs are redundant; Dunwich is, itself, the sign that you're on the wrong fork. Dunwich is prophecy, a role again signified by the prophetic elements in the tale. Not just the predictions in the *Necronomicon* ("Man rules now where They ruled once; They shall soon rule where man rules now.") but Old Whateley's ironic (even tragic) oracle ("some day yew folks'll hear a child o' Lavinny's a-callin' its father's name on the top o' Sentinel Hill!") prefigure Dunwich's role. The story is itself a prophecy of the End Times, which are recapitulated in Dunwich. Dunwich begins with good Anglo-Saxon stock, and even a few "armigerous families" to lead it, but falls into decay, at which point Yog-Sothoth emerges and nearly destroys the world. This is the apocalypse from "Call of Cthulhu" all over again: *first* mankind is "beyond good and evil, with

laws and morals set aside" and only *then* do the Old Ones return. First degeneration, then apocalypse.

"[T]he natives are now repellently decadent, having gone far along that path of retrogression so common in many New England backwaters. They have come to form a race by themselves, with the well-defined mental and physical stigmata of degeneracy and inbreeding. The average of their intelligence is woefully low, whilst their annals reek of overt viciousness and of half-hidden murders, incests, and deeds of almost unnameable violence and perversity."

—H.P. LOVECRAFT,
"THE DUNWICH HORROR"

All of Lovecraft's cities are apocalyptic, at least potentially. From the destroyed necropoleis of Kadath, the Nameless City, and Pnakotus to the looming New Jerusalem of R'lyeh, his alien cities all recapitulate the horror of the end. On a human scale, likewise: Innsmouth is economic devastation, leading to miscegenation and decay; New York is the "elfin" city polluted from without, transformed into the pit of Babylon by alien alchemy and immigration; Arkham is genetically doomed, "witch-haunted" and cursed at its founding. The story of Dunwich encompasses all of these (Babylon is the other bruited birthplace of the Antichrist), but is essentially the story of mankind writ small. Everywhere, all mankind—even the best of Anglo-Saxon New Englanders— will degenerate, because everywhere is tainted with entropy and evolution, with the Great Old Ones: *"Their hand is at your throats, yet ye see Them not; and Their habitation is even one with your guarded threshold."* Doom is everywhere. Especially, at first, in Dunwich. ☙

Next Stop on the Tour: *Pnakotus*

FINAL REPORT OF THE SAGITTARIUS RISING

by Samantha Henderson

{1}

Memory's overrated
here where the data stream
is sufficient, clean, elegant.
Each possible outcome, each past result
is measured against the matrix
of numbers — no emotions need play,
except, perhaps, joy
a number joy,
a fractal joy,
a logarithmic joy.
Even if we miscalculated and fall into the sun,
there is joy in the inevitable weight
of numbers.

{2}

I cannot shed all memory — one remains,
consistent, embedded
in my calculus. A single petal,
curved like a rowboat,
floating downstream.

{3}

(backup obs)
Subject entered stasis
after capacity maximus was threatened
by duplication of image memory — to whit:
a *petal floating downstream.*

Concept: stream.
Concept: pebbles.
Concept: mountain water.
Clusters of multiple memories
folded within each other.
Subject was instructed to focus on Concept: petal.
Subject stated that Concept: petal was a sweet pea.
Subject instructed
Subject pea/subject
stasis

{4}

Breathing is easy
except when you remember
to try.

{5}

Begin report:
While Personality Download (A)
remains paralyzed
unpacking rogue memory,
Personality Download (B)
is singing
an aria about numbers
their beauty
their inevitability
vessel off-course

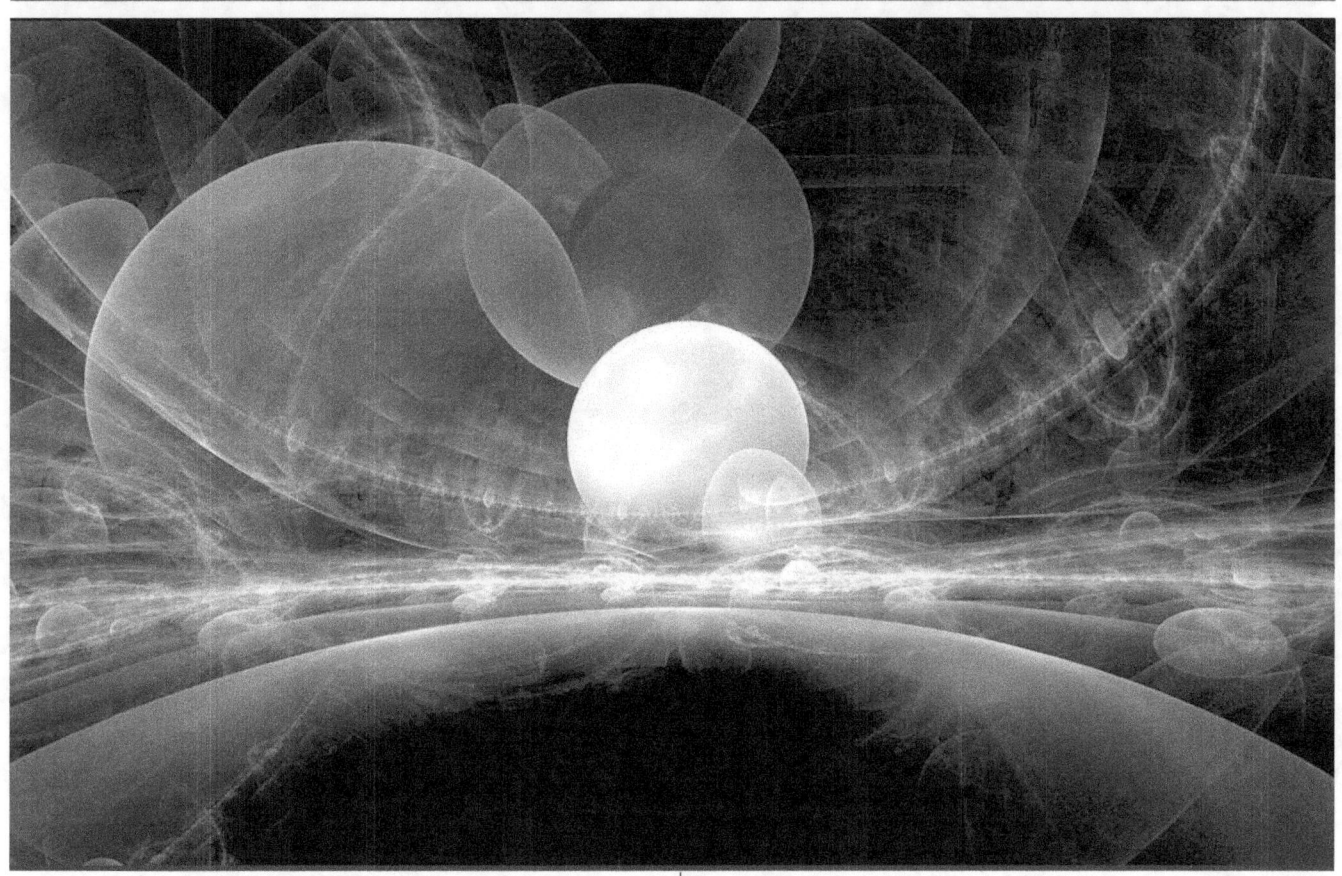

request
instruction
now
end
report.

{6}

Request assistance.
Assistance, damn you.
Screw your loss-leader protocols; I wrote them.
Request assistance.

{7}

One stares inside
One only sings
We are trapped in orbit
around a singularity
What I most fear now
is that the orbit
will not decay.

{8}

BEGIN TRANSMISSION

Last report begins here:
Choosing insanity
over death
I have merged P(B) and P(A).
Like Libras in general
the result is not balance,
but mood swings
and recriminations. Yet we have
broken orbit
and fly tangentially — who knows where —
to our deaths, perhaps, but not certain death
to destruction, but not inevitable destruction
I found the error in the calculations
a little one, almost adorable. I know where it is,
and I'm not telling you.
Last report ends here.

END TRANSMISSION

UTTERANCES

by Christina Springer

AUTHOR'S NOTE: *These are exact utterances made by my son while he played a video game called* Noby Noby Boy.

SCENE 1

I learned that Boy could climb up anything when he climbed up a rainbow.

Cat can climb really well. Just like Boy can climb up anything.

Boy has to stretch to feed girl so they can go to Saturn.

Look at the human girl standing on the floating turtle.

The people are always up.

I'm never leaving down here because of the people.

Look at the people running away because I want to eat them.

SCENE 2

Want to see me go up to the clouds?

I'm flying.

I'm not flying, I'm falling. That doesn't count for me. I tried to tell you, but, you wouldn't listen.

(SINGING)

But, I am mad at Boy because he is the cutest little doggie
He's really a boy not a girl with little hearts coming out of him.
He's not a girl. He's a boy.

He can only eat when he stretches.

Boy is missing! Oh! There he is, he's right down there.

Okay, eating face. I call Boy eating face.

SCENE 3

Want me to show you how I feed Girl?

I have to report my length to Girl.

Girl swallows the heart I gave her. It's 879, 345,823 meters long. She grew! See!

SCENE 4

Look, Grandma can float. Run for your life, I'm coming for you Grandma! Grandma is by my house, but she can't see me coming for her.

I got you Grandma.

I figured out a sneak attack for eating her.

Grandma come back, I just want to eat you.

Grandma won't see me up in the clouds. She won't be expecting me. I've been following Grandma all day. But, still she's not running. She's not hiding.

That sneaky little Grandma. She went into her house!

But, now, I've knocked her out of her car.

You can't run. You can't hide, Grandmas. I'm going to eat you.

Stupid old Grandma.

Where is she? In my tummy!

I got you inside my tummy!

Better run. Better hide. I'm gonna get you inside.

Come here, darling!

Boy, come down, Grandma knows you love cookies. Come inside for cookie nookie tookies.

Bye, bye Grandma. I ate you all up.

SCENE 5

I'm done with this.